NEMESIS AND THE VAULT OF LOST TIME

BY

P.J. DAVIS

"Wonder is the beginning of wisdom."

Socrates

To all who wonder…

CHAPTER 1

"**M**ax! Snap out of it! You're spacing out again!" The booming voice shocked Max into action. He bolted upright in his seat, trying to focus on the face looming in front of him. Beady, black pupils probed him like a giant insect inspecting its prey.

For a moment it seemed as if it were only a familiar nightmare until Ms. Stolty boomed again, "Perhaps if you would quit staring out the window, sniffling and sneezing, drifting off and daydreaming, you might actually find the time to complete your exam like the rest of the class!"

Muffled laughter echoed around the classroom. Max eyed the smirking faces and cringed. It wasn't as if he had committed a crime. All he had done was drift off for a minute during....

The test!

"It's a shame, Mr. Kellerman," Ms. Stolty said, frowning, her fleshy cheeks flapping back and forth. "Nearly every question you answer is correct. Now, if you could stop zoning out long enough to finish the *entire* test, you might actually live up to your potential! After all, it *is* your mid-term!" Ms. Stolty snatched Max's exam before he could even remove his pencil, scoring a dark, diagonal slash across the page, as if to underscore his failing.

Bzzzzzzzzzzzzz! The sound of the bell ended the longest fourth period in history.

"We'll discuss this later," Stolty warned.

"Hey, nice work there, Kellerman!"

Max groaned inwardly. Just the sort of response he'd expect from Kyle Saunders, the only seventh grader with a driver's license.

"But hey, at least you didn't drool down your sleeve like last week!"

"Ignore him, he's a total butthead," came the voice from the desk behind Max. It was Sam, his fifth period lab partner. She gave a

1

sympathetic nod as she passed by, carefully avoiding the crush of students pushing and elbowing their way through the door.

Ms. Stolty was last to exit, head tilted back, nose high, making it a point to flip the lights off as if nobody remained in the room. Tiny specks of dust floated aimlessly in a shaft of late afternoon light. Max breathed a deep sigh and gathered up his books, backpack, and large collection of tightly wadded tissues strewn about his desktop.

Okay, so maybe I do drift off, he thought. *And maybe I do "space out" at times, but sneezing and sniffling? How does that qualify as wasting time? And even so, I can't help the sneezing part!* Max could back up his statement with hard facts. He was a walking Wikipedia of obscure facts that he hoped would pay off some day when asked the final question on a TV game show of his choosing.

"So, Mr. Kellerman," the game host would say, "you hail from Providence, Rhode Island? Luckytown!" Max would nod politely. "For ten million dollars, approximately what percentage of the Earth's population sneezes when looking into direct sunlight?" Max would cock his head and pause for a moment, as the studio audience leaned forward in suspense. Then he would calmly and confidently reply, "Sir, that would have to be twenty-five to thirty-three percent!"

The surprised yet insincere game show host would turn to the audience and declare, "Well, that's correct, young man!" The crowd would gasp, clapping wildly at Max's vast reservoir of knowledge. And so as not to appear outdone, the host would read from his notecard and ask, "I don't suppose you know what causes this reaction?"

"Actually, I do," Max would reply with attractive modesty. "It's because some people have nerve endings in their noses that are connected to the nerves in their eyes in such a way that it causes them—no, actually it *makes* them—sneeze."

The host's mouth would then gape open in amazement, and the crowd would erupt again in cheers. Ms. Stolty would, of course, be the first to announce the news. "I always knew Max had it in him, such an exceptionally bright young man," she would say. "I always said he had potential…." And *blah-de-blah-de-blah* it would go, with everyone nodding in agreement that Max had finally discovered an actual use for his potential.

But for now, that just wasn't so. Max slipped out the classroom door and into a moving wall of bodies. Music blared everywhere, locker doors slammed shut, and shouts bounced about the hallway. An unmanned skateboard whizzed past, nearly wiping out two other students as they ran to beat the next bell. Max hurried as well, even though band was his next subject; Mr. Scottsburg wouldn't care if he were late since he was rarely on time himself. Max pushed against the double doors that led into the vast, windowless music room and worked his way through the tiers of outstretched legs, untied shoes, and fallen music stands. Finding his usual seat in the wind section, he slid his overstuffed backpack under his chair and opened his alto saxophone case.

Whack! Max felt an open-handed smack on the back.

"You were so busted!" his best friend, Derek, laughed.

"It's not that funny," Max grumbled as he slipped the strap of his trusty sax around his neck. "And besides, I'll still make an eighty-five anyway and get at least a B-plus. Can you match that, Mr. 'Can-I-study-with-you-the-night-before-the-test'?"

"Hey! I had other options," Derek insisted. "I just wanted to help *you* brush up. Anyway, what's with the sneezing fit and the dazed look in class? You are in serious need of sleep. Even Sam noticed it, dude, and she sits *behind* you!"

Max bit down on his bottom lip, replaying the event in his mind. "It could be that photic sneeze reflex, what some people call the 'ACHOO syndrome,' that genetic thing I told you about when the sunlight stimulates the nerve endings in the nose, making you sneeze. Or it could just be allergies, which would explain the tiredness, and you know how that makes Ms. Stolty go crazy—"

"Max!" Derek interrupted, looking bewildered.

"You're not following this, are you?"

"Actually? No, not a word."

"Okay, how to put this?" Max paused to collect his thoughts. "Derek, do you ever feel like you are going right along, and then suddenly your brain freezes, like it's on pause? Sort of like the rainbow wheel on the computer, just spinning but going nowhere?"

"What?" Derek questioned, one eyebrow raised slightly higher in disbelief. "Um…? No?"

"Really? 'Cause sometimes I get this glitch-y feeling, like time stops for a minute, then suddenly starts up again. Like today, I'm taking that test one minute and suddenly everyone's staring, and Ms. Stolty pops up out of nowhere. Not sure just how that happens."

"Could just be that your noodle is cooked," Derek replied. "It's like eating pizza and Twinkies and then playing video games all night. It leaves you with that totally zoned-out feeling." Derek bit down hard on a Granny Smith apple he had scavenged from his backpack, spraying a perfect arc of apple juice across Max's instrument case, while hitting Max in one eye. Max winced, shaking his head. Derek had the unusual knack of transforming a simple question into a baffling answer. What's more, every response seemed to involve food—a subject never far from Derek's mind. But to Max, that wasn't important.

"Gotta question," said Max. "You've known me since second grade. How many times in the last five years have I ever copped a sugar buzz? I don't buy your theory."

"Well then, how about buying this?" Derek pulled his chair alongside Max's, swung the shiny bell of his new trombone up to Max's left ear, and gave it a blast.

"Hey! That ear has to last me a lifetime!" Max's voice echoed inside his head. Derek gave Max one more blast for effect.

"Okay, man, so you're freaked out because you have some weird sneeze disorder or you tend to zone out in class, big deal! And sure, you get busted now and then for going comatose, or whatever it is that you do. Practically everyone does it once in a while. Ease up."

Max sighed. "I guess you're right. But it's happening a lot lately, and I can't seem to stop it."

* * *

The doorway bell chimed brightly as Max entered his uncle's bookstore. It sat tucked away in a modest row of shops in the College Hill area of Providence. For Max it was a home away from home. The smell of musty paperbacks and polished oak floors held all the comfort of a nicely worn blanket.

"Hey, Max! Great, you're just in time!" a muffled voice rang out from below the front counter.

"Uncle Owen? Where are—"

Max's uncle popped up suddenly from behind the frosted glass counter, releasing a plume of dust from a carton of unsorted novels. He squinted as he read the title of each one, mumbling and nodding, as if recalling an old acquaintance. "Do you have a minute?"

"Sure," Max replied willingly as he surveyed the countertop for the ceramic dish of York Peppermint Patties left out for coffee-drinking patrons. It was all part of a daily ritual. Max had successfully petitioned his uncle on the importance of an afternoon snack to ward off low blood sugar. It was one of a number of perks that came with the job.

"Could you help me sort through this shipment of books? They're getting pretty stacked up back here."

"No problem," Max said, as he swung his heavy backpack off his shoulders and onto the floor behind the cash register counter. He gazed up at the faded colored spines of a thousand book jackets. They lined the towering shelves across from him, an endless treasure trove of obscure and exotic knowledge. Another whirl of dust stirred as he grabbed the first set of books from the cardboard box.

Achoo! Max sneezed abruptly. *Achoo! Achoo!* A package of tissues automatically slid toward him from across the counter.

"Thanks, Uncle Owen."

"Hey, I met an interesting man today," his uncle said as he tucked a tattered romance novel into its proper place. "A German physicist whose ancestors once lived in a castle near Heidelberg. His name's Von Guttenberg—Dr. Hans Von Guttenberg. How's that for a name? He was searching through some of those old out-of-print books I salvaged out of your father's basement storage room. Figured it was about time. Intriguing gentleman." Max ran a cloth across a long, empty shelf in preparation for more books.

Achoo!

"Sorry!" Max said sheepishly.

"Don't be," his uncle said, turning to locate another full box. It didn't surprise Max that his uncle met so many interesting people, since the bookstore was a magnet for odd characters. One man was planning to build a life-size replica of Noah's Ark and use it as a combination zoo and museum. Another lady claimed she had set the Guinness World Record for reading eighty-four books out loud and backwards in pig Latin.

"So what was this guy looking for, Uncle Owen?"

"Well, funny you should ask. He said he was studying the phenomenon known as déjà vu."

"Déjà vu? Sounds more like French than German."

"It *is* French. It means the illusion that something you're experiencing for the first time has happened before. It happens to everyone at some point."

Max stopped to think for a moment. "You mean that weird feeling when something happens, but you could swear it's some kind of slow-motion mental replay?"

"Yes, but that's just it… you haven't actually thought of it before, it just seems that way, a trick of the imagination."

"*Or so they say…*" Max half wondered, half muttered out loud.

"I'm sorry, what was the question?" Uncle Owen inquired, cocking his head slightly to the side to hear better.

"Oh nothing," Max insisted. "Just curious as to why this guy was researching that particular subject?"

"It seems Von Guttenberg has a notion that it's no illusion at all. A bit of pseudoscience nonsense, if you ask me, but it takes all kinds." His uncle tried to squeeze *Beekeeping for Dummies* into a narrow slot at the end of the shelf. "It just won't fit," he said, gritting his teeth and pushing harder.

"Give it here, Uncle Owen," Max said. "How about if I put that on the display table in the back?"

His uncle nodded. "And while you're at it, clear a spot for homework."

Max went off to the reading room at the back of the store and placed the oversized book in the center of the table, alongside a volume on advanced origami. He paused, marveling at the diverse subjects lining the shelves around him. NASCAR racing, the Great Wall of China, humpback whales, small engine repair, dark energy—the topics seemed endless.

As he turned to leave, Max noticed another title, handwritten and taped over the cover of a tattered, leather-bound book on a small reading table in the corner of the room. He moved closer to make certain he had read the cover correctly. *Nemesis and the Vault of Lost Time.* Max glanced around the room, checking to see if anyone had been reading the book and perhaps had left it laying out for reference. But the room appeared empty. He pulled a chair up close to the table to get a better look. The binding was fragile, its thumb-worn pages brown with age. Gently he turned the book's cover open to peer inside. There, on the first page, someone had transcribed a short note in the margins. The penmanship was crisp and angular with a forward slant to it. The ink was a deep blue and more recent, compared to the older text, which had faded over time, making it nearly illegible. Curious, he read the note out loud.

> "As the Earth revolves, each breath grows shorter. The daylight dims and the shadows lengthen. Things once imagined appear to be, when time releases those from the deep."

Max squinted to make sure he was reading the handwriting correctly. He tilted the book forward to see more clearly in the light when he felt a bony hand grasp his right shoulder.

Chapter 2

"It's a translation," the thick German accent sounded from behind him. Max spun around in his chair, nearly falling backwards. He looked up at a thin, elderly gentleman dressed in a brown tweed jacket, one hand on a glossy, hand-carved wooden cane, the other extended out towards Max.

"I... I didn't see anyone else here," Max stammered.

"I know," said the man with a smile. "I can be as quiet as a church mouse. Von Guttenberg's the name. Dr. Hans von Guttenberg, but most people call me Professor Gutt." He smiled again, head tilted slightly to the right, staring first at Max and then at the book in his hands. "So you noticed the manuscript, did you?"

Max paused, glanced down at the book, and offered up an awkward half smile, not knowing if the old man's comment was meant as an observation or an accusation. "I... I just thought the title looked interesting, that's all."

"Interesting? Hmm... I never really quite thought of it as 'interesting'." Professor Gutt stroked his thin, white beard as he pondered the description. Leaning closer, he cupped his long, weathered fingers and whispered into Max's ear, "I think of it more as appalling, shocking, deeply disturbing, something that should demand the attention of national leaders, world governments, the United Nations, perhaps." Then he sighed heavily, pulled away, and gently lowered himself onto a nearby wooden chair. "But it's hard to prove the world's most important substance is missing when no one knows it's gone."

"Substance? What substance?" Max asked.

"Time itself!" exclaimed the old man. "And it's being sucked out of this planet at a faster pace every day." The professor whirled his cane about wildly as he spoke. "It's all there in that book. It's been known about for centuries but just not proven. Meanwhile the levels in the Vault just keep growing higher and higher…" he said, his voice trailing off.

"What vault?" Max insisted before realizing the abrupt nature of his question. "What I meant was, what exactly is this vault?"

"Why… The Vault of Lost Time! The Tank of Tears! The Well of Immortality! However you want to describe the massive cauldron of trillions upon trillions of stolen seconds. And now they want this book—because of what it represents."

"What *what* represents?" Max asked, now completely confused, and yet focused on nothing but the man's next statement.

"The way to stop it! The way to get it back!" he said, again lowering his voice to a whisper. "You see, Max, this book contains stories, maps, and clues, repeated over the centuries and throughout countless cultures, about a realm not far from ours where hideous creatures have been systematically harvesting time from the lives of humans."

"Harvesting? Do you mean they're *stealing* it?"

"Precisely."

"Why would they do that?" Max asked.

"To increase their life force! So that someday… and not too far in the future if my calculations are correct, they can enter our world and destroy it. And that's only the beginning." Professor Guttenberg again leaned toward Max, with one eye bulging slightly farther out than the other. "This place would be nothing more than a rest stop!"

Is this guy for real? Creatures? Lost vault? Or just some kind of whack case?

Max studied the deep creases etched across the old man's face. He was looking for any signs that the Professor was putting him on, but there was no tell-tale twinkle, no hint of a smirk. Not even a whiff of alcohol. No, this Von Guttenberg character appeared to be completely convinced of everything he said. Max nervously eyed the doorway, racking his brain for a polite excuse to exit before the professor started talking about UFOs and meeting flesh-eating aliens.

"Max, I know this must sound like the ramblings of a doddering old man. I'm not asking you to believe a word I've said. Just read the book for yourself and form your own conclusions. But once your eyes are opened, you will realize it's happening all around us. They're stealing time, and if it doesn't stop, it'll be gone... for all of us." He pressed the manuscript firmly against Max's chest. "I can't pursue it any longer. I'm getting too old, and it will take a younger heart and a determined mind to go any further. Every shred of evidence I've researched points toward the existence of this realm, this netherworld, but none of it is as complete as the book you now hold in your hands. That's why it's special. Those on the other side want to keep it from mortals like you and me. They feed on ignorance. It allows them to operate undetected so they can continue to increase their power and ultimately invade our world—for theirs is a desolate place! Greed always seeks more. And that's why they're stealing from us, second by second, minute by minute, lifetime by lifetime. But the moment is coming when they will use it. Some call it Armageddon, the end of the world. And if the Vault is not emptied... well, it's not a question of if, but when."

"Max!" a voice rang out. It was Uncle Owen. "Almost time to close up. Are you finished back there?" Max looked back at the old man.

"Go," he motioned. "Take the book, it really belongs to you, in more ways than one. Study the maps, read the notations, and try to open your mind to it, Max. I have tried for a lifetime to find a way in and so have others—in fact, someone very much like you. That's what brought me back here. I have no one left to see this through. But I must warn you: There are those who will try to stop you—changelings. They aren't who they appear to be, Max, and you mustn't trust them." His stern look softened as he studied Max's expression.

"I do see the resemblance," he uttered quietly, looking deeply into Max's eyes, as if confirming a suspicion.

"Wait," Max insisted, putting up his hand for a moment as if to take a verbal time out. "What exactly do you mean by changelings? And a resemblance to what?"

With that, the professor slowly stood up and straightened his stiff back. "I wish I could tell you this was all some fairy tale, Max, but it's not. These forces may not be visible now, but that doesn't make them any less real. No less real than time itself."

Max looked down at the book he was now holding in his hands and felt his head reeling from all the old man had revealed to him. "How could any of this be possible?" he wondered. Not knowing what to say, he turned back and said, "I... I'm just not sure what you want me to—" But the professor was gone.

"Max! We're closing up early tonight. Let's get going," his uncle yelled from the front of the store.

"Sure, just a minute." Max hesitated for a moment, before walking over to check the back door. Hearing the click of the lock, Max turned, unzipped his book bag, and carefully placed the weathered book inside. He scanned the aisles of books once more for any sign of the professor. *Quiet as a church mouse...* Flipping the lights off, he turned and walked quickly through the darkened storefront to meet his uncle.

"Are you alright there, Max?" his uncle asked once they were inside the car.

"Yeah, I just have a lot of homework to do yet," Max replied, weighing whether he should mention his encounter.

"Uncle Owen..." He paused for a second.

"Yes," his uncle replied with a tilt of the head.

"The professor you mentioned, had you ever met him before? I mean... did he say where he was from? Or how he came to find your bookstore?"

"Hmmm, well no, not that I recall," Uncle Owen responded, scratching the side of his beard, as if to help him think. "I would have remembered meeting a character like that." His voice trailed off as he processed Max's question, then pausing for a moment, mumbled lightly, "Although he did mention teaching in Zurich."

"Teaching? In Zurich? As in ETH Zurich? The university where…"

"What??" his uncle replied suddenly, as if he had misspoken.

"Wait! Did you ask him if he knew—"

"N-no!" Uncle Owen insisted, shaking his head side to side. "Probably just a coincidence. Anyway, I thought you said you had all kinds of homework," Uncle Owen said, changing the subject.

"Yeah… yeah I do," Max acknowledged begrudgingly, slumping back down in his seat. He sighed inwardly.

Nothing makes sense.

Max stared out the window as they drove. His outstretched hands felt the crackled texture of the worn leather seats. Lightly rubbing his open palms across the rough surface felt comforting and grounding in a way that was hard to explain. They continued the short route to the narrow, two-story clapboard house on the south end of Benefit Street where Max lived with his mother. The rows of houses blurred together as they drove along. Streetlights and a light misty rain highlighted the wet pavement. Max texted Derek and they agreed to meet at 8:00 p.m. *Better yet,* he thought, *text Sam as well.* Derek could be counted on for his hot takes, but Sam was his voice of reason. He'd have to wait another hour to get their second opinions. Meanwhile, the questions kept repeating.

The vault? Nemesis? A resemblance? To whom *or what?*

CHAPTER 3

"The guy sounds like a freak, if you ask me," Derek said matter-of-factly. "Maybe he's a writer that got fired from the SciFi Channel or he escaped from that mental hospital for the criminally insane. You know, the one over in Cranston where that guy got loose and ate six kids in his neighborhood?"

"Yeah, yeah," Max said, trying not to roll his eyes. The last time Derek told that story, the mental hospital was in Warwick and the man ate only three kids. Max kept staring down at the manuscript, ignoring Derek's grotesque hypothesis.

"I don't believe that's true," Sam intervened, her blue-green eyes narrowing intently as she closely inspected the manuscript.

"What, you don't believe this guy ate six kids?" Derek said defensively. "Okay, so maybe it was just five, unless they counted a pet...."

"No," Sam continued, "I mean, I don't believe the old man in the store was crazy. And even though he made some unbelievable claims, he seemed to know what he was talking about. And what's the chance he also taught in Zurich?"

"Let me get this straight," Derek said, shooting a look at Sam and then staring back at Max in amazement. "You talked to this guy for all of ten minutes, and he tells you that time is ending or some mysterious pot of gobbledygook is going to boil over. And now you act as though he's some Einstein, like Elon Musk, or the genius who invented Pop Tarts?"

"Mm-hmm," Max said, nodding his head slowly in agreement to Sam's initial assessment. He had blocked out nearly everything Derek had said and instead turned his attention back to the manuscript.

"Let's see that again," Max requested, as Sam handed him back the manuscript. Throughout its yellowed pages, hand-scrawled notes filled the linings. Despite the age of the text, some of the handwritten notations looked more recent, freshly penned and strangely familiar.

As the Earth revolves, each breath grows shorter. The daylight dims and the shadows lengthen. Things once imagined appear to be, when time releases those from the deep.

Max flipped ahead, scanning the pages carefully, all the while mumbling to himself. "He might not be Einstein, but he's probably not as 'cray cray' as you say he is. It's hard to verify his story, since this book is written in a foreign language."

"What language do you think it is?" Sam inquired, peering over his shoulder.

"Not any I recognize. Looks similar to French and Spanish and everything in between. Someone translated bits and pieces into English here in the margins. Same with the book title, it's taped over with an English translation."

Derek edged up in curiosity and peered in as well. They all took the same French class though Derek only remembered the words *baguette* and *croissant.*

"I give up," Derek said, shaking his head. "You'd need a United Nations translator to figure this mess out."

"Hey! Not a bad idea!" Max said.

"What?"

"We'll just use a translator and then go from there."

"But aren't those people expensive?" Derek objected. "And who do you know who translates? Besides, how can you be sure they'll know this particular language?"

"Who said anything about hiring a translator? We can just use something online." Max reached up to his desk and grabbed his laptop, typing a short burst of characters.

"Here we go. This app should be able to autodetect the language and translate it all at once." With the manuscript propped open at his side, Max typed in the first sentence he saw. He pressed ENTER and waited. Within seconds, the answer came back.

"Latin?" Sam said with a puzzled look. "That's a bit strange."

"Hmm… strange, yes, but that's also why it looks so familiar. Most romance languages like French, Italian, Spanish, and Portuguese are based on Latin." Max bit his lower lip thoughtfully.

"But who writes in Latin nowadays?" Derek injected. "And besides that, how did this fossil of a book get in your family's bookstore?"

"First of all, hardly anyone writes in Latin anymore. It's a dead language," Sam insisted. "But that doesn't mean people still don't study it."

Max nodded in agreement. "Sam's right, and apparently someone was studying this particular Latin in great detail."

"But why? Who'd study a dead language? Vampires? Morticians?"

Max and Sam rolled their eyes in unison.

"Most likely people like Professor Gutt, or anyone interested in decoding old texts."

"Yeah, like when they deciphered the writings on the Rosetta Stone," Sam chimed in. "That helped unlock all kinds of clues to ancient civilizations."

Max grinned inwardly. He appreciated Sam's fellow geekiness. They had all volunteered at Rhode Island's Summer Academy for Interactive Learning. She led the reading program, Max helped organize field trips to the local aquarium and planetarium, and Derek coached pickleball.

Derek remained unimpressed. "So, in other words, the only people who care about this stuff are crazy types and word nerds like you two?"

"Nerds?" Max objected. "I prefer 'well informed,' and besides, I can't help that I was raised in a bookstore by a theoretical mathematician and brainwashed nightly by a school librarian." Derek and Sam laughed in agreement, while Max managed a reluctant grin.

"Anyway, to address your second question, this book most likely came from a box lot at an estate auction. You should remember those trips, Derek."

"You mean like the ones with you and Mr. K when we all went to Pawtucket?"

"Yes, exactly." Max nodded, reflecting on the memory. "Like the one where you scored the mood ring for a buck-fifty."

"Alright, alright, you go ahead and laugh, but how's that any worse than your hourglass collection? At least I know how I'm feeling. See?" Derek pointed to his right index finger. "My mood ring says I'm getting hungry."

"Well, you two boys have at it, I'm calling it a night," Sam said. "Let me know what you find out, Max. Maybe the old professor will turn up again at the bookstore. I'll do a little research and see what I can find out about him online." Max nodded in appreciation. With that, Sam slung her book bag over her shoulder, fist bumped them both, and headed out.

"Check the mini-fridge, Derek. I think there's pizza bagels."

"Now we're talking," Derek replied.

Derek nuked three bagels and nearly burned his mouth while biting the first one.

"You couldn't wait all of fifteen seconds?" Max shook his head.

"Told you I was hungry. So, what did that program say about the mystery writings? Any chance there's a treasure map?"

"Not likely…" Max replied as he copy-pasted the translated text section by section into a new word doc. "And besides, why would you even need the money?"

"Wait! What are you saying?" Derek objected.

It amazed Max that Derek received a sizable allowance for doing nothing but studying and getting passable grades—an arrangement Max referred to as "teenage retirement."

"Okay, here goes." Max scrolled back to the first page of the translated doc and zoomed in. Derek edged in closer as Max read it out loud.

From those who guard the eternal truths,
May our lives protect the souls of man.
We pledge to free the captured past
And seal our world from those who've strayed.

Underneath was a list of 126 names, all carefully signed, as if part of a sworn oath.

"Hey, check this out," Derek said, pointing to the reference that followed the signatures:

The Benedictine Order
Paris, y. 1478

Max thought for a moment, tapping his keyboard lightly, as if to help speed his mental processing. "Benedictine? Hmmm… as in the Benedictine monks?" He glanced over at Derek for confirmation.

Derek eyebrows raised in surprise. "You're asking me?"

"Yeah!" Max insisted. "Don't you remember reading about medieval monks in Stolty's class last semester? A lot of them served as scribes."

"Scribes as in scribble or scrabble, is that from Latin, too?"

"Sort of, since there wasn't a printing press at that time, it was up to scribes to preserve all knowledge by copying books by hand."

"Wait, I thought copying books was plagiarism." Derek laughed before realizing the stern look on Max's face. "So how does copying books connect them to some underworld, Max, I still don't get it. Come on, just type in some more stuff from the book."

Max sighed. "This will take too long. I have a better idea…"

Max leapt up and onto the swivel chair by his desk. Flipping the manuscript open, he placed it face down on his scanner. For the next half hour Max scanned the pages, converting them into image files, and finally into one big text file. Once finished, he uploaded the final text file into the translation app. Max read it hungrily while Derek laid sprawled in a beanbag chair, playing a hand-held video game.

"So?" Derek casually asked Max, not bothering to look up from his game.

"So… what?" Max said, still staring intently at the final page of the translated manuscript.

"So, what's the deal? Does it back up professor what's-his-name's story? Or does it just read like those English Lit assignments with a bunch of thee's and thou's?" Derek said, dropping his chin, speaking in a deep English accent.

"Both," Max replied matter-of-factly, swinging back around in his chair and staring directly at Derek, as if to force his full attention.

Sensing his tone, Derek abruptly sat up, tossed his controller to the side, and turned, locking eyes with Max.

"Wait! You mean there's *actually* something to it? Like what?"

Max leaned in farther and continued in a hushed tone, as if aware of the secretive nature of the information. "Well, according to this manuscript, there *were* these creatures who stole life energy, in the form of time, by siphoning it out of people when they least suspected it."

"So, for real… time-sucking creatures?" Derek asked with piqued interest.

"Sucking, stealing, hoarding—whatever you want to call it. And the entities that harvested the time lived in a place known as Nemesis—which is some sort of netherworld, like a dimensional holding pen. It's not entirely clear."

"Whoa!" Derek exclaimed.

"Right?" echoed Max, nodded in full agreement, glad to see he finally had Derek's undivided attention. "And it gets better. It seems they stole the time from humans hoping to supercharge their own life force."

Derek wrinkled his nose in question. "Creatures? Entities? That doesn't give us much to go by, does it?"

"Actually, it says the creatures who stole time were known as Boggarts, and they were like bankers. They collected the time, stored it, and accounted for each second."

"Does it say who they gave it to?"

"Most of it went directly into..." Max paused, flipping the translated page around to face Derek, revealing a sentence fragment highlighted in bright yellow marker.

"...a central vault!"

Max caught Derek's bewildered stare.

"Wow! It's just like the old guy said, Max. Man, this is getting super weird!"

"It goes on to say a portion of the life force, which they called *prana,* was distributed to a whole list of characters... shapeshifters, wereboars, imps, hobgoblins, fiends, sprites, pixies, poltergeists..."

Derek was now so intrigued by the unfolding story that he momentarily forgot that he'd already decided none of this could be true. "Okay, but how did they get this time to start with?"

"That's the really interesting part," Max said, shuffling pages back and forth, as if piecing together a torn ransom note. "They stole it when people were most vulnerable. Like during the split-second when someone sneezed. Apparently, people were more aware of these things back then and sensed it."

Max paused to let the information fully sink in.

"It actually makes sense," Max thought out loud. "That might be why the Germans would say *Gesundheit,* which means 'good health'—perhaps they realized a second of life had just been snatched away. And the English said, 'God bless you' probably for the same reason—hoping to ward off any evil."

Derek sat back, trying to guess how many times he had sneezed in all his thirteen years.

"It goes on to say that you can see into this realm when you daydream," Max went on, "but you can't enter it. And before you come back, the Boggarts erase any knowledge of what you've just seen and replace it with a recent memory. The Benedictine Monks of France describe it as... *déjà vu*."

Max stopped, remembering the phrase his uncle had told him earlier that afternoon. *The illusion that something you're experiencing has happened before...*

"This is getting sketchy, Max," Derek cautioned. "Maybe you should just take the book back to the store or burn it or donate it to Goodwill or something. If this were my house, my mom would toss it and sage the place."

Max felt the same strange uneasiness. "I would, but that old professor today... he said *others* were trying to find this information. If what's in here is true, I don't want to even think about who or what might be searching for added lifetimes."

Buzzzzzzzz, buzzzzzzz.

Max glanced over to see his phone vibrating.

"Who'd be calling you now?" Derek asked skeptically. "It's way too late for telemarketers."

"No idea, it says 'UNKNOWN'."

"If it's important, they can leave a message."

"Maybe that's what this is," Max muttered, recalling the day's odd events, "a message. I left the professor my number in case he had more information."

"You did what?!" Derek exclaimed in disbelief.

Ignoring Derek, Max hit the speaker button on his phone.

"Hello, Max," announced the strangely garbled voice before Max could even speak.

"H-hello?" he replied, puzzled by the odd, vibrating quality of the caller's voice. "Professor...?"

"We are looking for a book, one that may have fallen into your possession. Perhaps you found it in your uncle's bookstore?"

"Wait? Who is this?" Max shot back.

"Who we are needn't concern you or your friend, Max. We just want the book back."

"What do you know about me… and how did you get this number?"

"We know a lot, Max. About you, about the book, and especially about what happened to the old man who gave it to you. You wouldn't want the same unfortunate things that happened to him to happen to you… or to your friend, now, would you, Max?"

"What?" Derek suddenly injected. "I don't know what kind of sick joke you think you're playing," he said, his voice rising higher in pitch, "but if you stole this guy's phone and you think some stupid prank call is going to scare us…"

"Scare? Oh, I'm afraid you don't even know the meaning of the word. But if you don't return the book to the store by tomorrow, you soon will."

CHAPTER 4

"**Y**ou look like death warmed over!"

Max woke up with a start to see his mom standing over him, shaking her head.

"Do you have *any* idea how late you two stayed up last night? Two o'clock in the morning! And you wonder why you're falling asleep during a pop quiz. Now, get cracking. There's eggs and sausage waiting on the table. And just what kind of report is it that's got you working this hard?" Her voice trailed off as she left his bedroom for the kitchen.

Max looked at the scattered pages of the translated text spread across the floor. Everywhere lay notes from sources he'd found and printed out: archived web sites, pdf's from research studies, reference books, old textbooks, and a dried out yellow highlighter. Derek gave up long before Max did and retreated to his house three doors down on the opposite side of the street. Now Max gathered up the papers and, squaring them neatly with a tap on the corner of the desk, placed them in a new folder from his supply drawer. The book itself he placed neatly inside an interior zippered pouch in his backpack, still mindful of last night's call and determined to keep it close at hand.

Slipping on his well-worn Patriots cap, he made his way to the kitchen. The warm morning sunlight and aroma of freshly scrambled sausage and eggs created a welcome contrast to the ominous events of the night before.

"Max, are you okay, honey?" his mom asked while dishing an oversized portion on his plate.

"Yeah, I'm just, you know, kind of under a lot of pressure right now." Max tried to be as vague as possible.

"What kind of pressure?" his mom inquired, pressing the question in order to get a better read of the situation. It was a librarian's nature to research, collecting sufficient evidence to justify her continual concern.

"I guess you could call it, deadlines, er—I mean time constraints." Max winced at the unintentional double meaning, hoping it wouldn't lead to further interrogation.

"Oh, okay. Well, I'm sure you'll figure it out," his mother replied with an air of relief. "Let me know if there is anything I can do to help. I know with the annual book fair going on at the library and the readings each night by all these guest authors, I've been a little caught up myself."

"That's alright, Mom," Max reassured her. This isn't something you could help with anyway,"

"Well, I can recommend a couple of good books on time management..."

"Really, it's okay," Max insisted. I'll just head over to the bookstore after school...."

Max interrupted himself mid-sentence. The voice on the phone had demanded the book be returned there. But Max wouldn't even know what the caller looked like—or what he might do. One thing was for sure—Max was not about to set foot back in that bookstore until he gathered more information, and that meant he needed a safe place to do his own research.

"On second thought, Mom, how about if I just head over to the library after school and help you with the book fair? The exhibit tables last year were pretty cool."

His mother looked up in surprise. Max cocked his head to the side and held his expression, not wanting to arouse suspicion. His mother knew he preferred his interactions with Uncle Owen over the hushed tones and strict rules of the library.

"Well, sure, honey, that would be fine," his mother nodded in approval. "I think you'll get a lot out of it. We have one author this year in particular who has written a fascinating book about medieval spells and myths. He even went to Europe on a sabbatical to research his findings."

Perfect! That way he would get two things done: avoid trouble and dig further into the contents of the manuscript. The library was just the place to hide out and hunker down. Max hurriedly finished his breakfast, placed the dishes in the sink, and jumped into the passenger seat of his mother's faded yellow Volvo station wagon.

* * *

The library on Hancock Street was just one block down from the school, but Max wasn't going to take any chances. He watched nervously as he hurried down the empty sidewalk and then ambled up the wide marble steps to the library's large glass double doors. Each side of the entrance was flanked by old statues of angelic figures so covered with moss and ivy they looked like hideous gargoyles. Max paused a moment before going inside, wondering for the umpteenth time that day if his imagination was just getting the better of him.

Probably, he thought.

He approached the main reception desk and spotted his mother arranging books on tables throughout the main floor in anticipation of the seven o'clock event.

"Max!" she exclaimed, still brimming with pleasure that he had indeed taken an interest in her book fair. "Could you be an angel and help Mr. Gabriel over there set up his presentation? Here's his name badge and welcome packet."

Max obliged and headed across the highly polished terrazzo floors, his footsteps echoing up past the balcony. Mr. Gabriel, a short and portly fellow, was busily arranging his books, pamphlets and a number of what looked like ceramic figurines, completely oblivious to Max's arrival.

Max paused for a moment. The plain gray folding table was now stuffed end-to-end so as to slightly bow from the weight of the merchandise. Behind it stood a dark blue felt display board with hand cut stencils standing out in yellow. On it, the author had pinned what appeared to be highly detailed drawings and artist renderings of impish creatures that resembled the figurines on the table. Max leaned in closer to look, just as Mr. Gabriel stepped back to admire his display—and promptly stepped on Max's left foot.

"Oh! I'm sorry!" Max winced, feeling a greater sense of agony than apology. After all, *he* didn't step on anyone's toes.

"Oh, no, I should apologize," Mr. Gabriel replied, grabbing Max firmly by the elbow to steady him. "I should look where I'm going! Can I help you with something, young man?"

"Actually, I'm here to help you. My mom over there is the head librarian, and I'm assisting her today. She thought you might need an extra set of hands." Max held out the welcome packet and clip-on name tag, which Mr. Gabriel eagerly took, pinning the label to his brown and blue tweed jacket with satisfaction.

"Great!" Mr. Gabriel exclaimed, pleased with the orderliness of his handiwork. Spinning back around he looked directly at Max, extended a thick and rather rough hand towards him, like a deacon greeting a newcomer to church.

"Well then, great, just great!" he repeated. "And you are Mr…?"

"Oh, it's just Max," Max insisted, feeling funny anytime an adult referred to him as a "Mister."

"Okay, Max, nice to meet you. I'm 'Mr.' Gabriel, but you can just call me Gabe for short, how's that?" Mr. Gabriel insisted, and he pumped Max's hand repeatedly with a surprisingly strong grip.

"And if you want to help, Max, you can just unload a few more of the books from the box under this table and stand them on end in front of the table, like this," he said demonstrating his technique. "Then I think we'll be all set!"

Max began lifting the heavy books out one by one, all the while keeping one eye on the fiendish figurines staring back at him from the table. They seemed to be saying, "Yep, we're *exactly* what you were reading about last night."

"I see you've taken a liking to them," Gabe smiled, noting Max's curious yet puzzled stare.

"I don't know if the word is 'like,'" Max said politely, "but they're definitely… different."

"No need to be diplomatic, Max," Gabe replied, "These things are just plain ugly—no two ways about it. But medieval literature is full of them."

"Who… I mean, *what* exactly are they?" Max asked, trying to make his interest sound as casual as possible.

"Just an assortment of creatures—gnomes, goblins, gremlins, you name it. They were as common then as, well, zombie movies are now," he said with a slight snort, as if caught off guard by his own sense of humor.

"By common, you don't mean *real*, do you?"

"That depends on your definition of 'real.'"

"Well, I guess I mean things you can touch and feel. Solid things."

Mr. Gabriel paused for a second, and stroking the short stubble of his salt and pepper beard, leaned toward Max. "Well, by that definition, are video games real? How about movies… or TV shows… superheroes? Some things 'live' in people's imagination. Others exist in what we call real life. And sometimes the lines get blurred." At that remark, Mr. Gabriel's eyes lit up, and grabbing one of the figurines in hand, held it up to Max's face for close viewing. Max snapped back his head in an attempt to focus on the ceramic carving, its tiny eyes bulging back at Max.

"What's important, what's worth noting, is that they were 'real' to the people back then." Mr. Gabriel paused again, raising one eyebrow higher, as if in deep thought. "Hmmm… maybe, real isn't even the right word. Back in the Dark Ages, people were more shall-we-say 'aware'— aware of a lot of things we aren't now."

"Really? Like what?" Max asked, quietly backing up a half step, listening all the more intently as he continued stacking books on the display tables.

"Well, for one, the presence of death. Remember, their time on Earth was very short, about half our current average lifetime. Scientists and historians blame it on the plagues and the crusades and malnutrition, but those were just the symptoms of what was an emerging, unfolding darkness."

Mr. Gabriel paused, eyeing Max's expression, as if to gauge whether Max was truly interested in his work, or just making conversation. Sensing Max's sincerity, he leaned forward, cupping his left hand to the side of his mouth, and whispered in Max's ear, as if sharing a closely guarded secret.

"Some even claim there were certain *forces* at work, draining the very life out of people. Exactly what these forces were, no one knew. All the royalty, and even the clergy, felt if something wasn't done to stop it, all humanity would soon die out."

Max pulled back, his eyebrows raised up before exclaiming in a not-so-hush tone, "Die out? What? So, what happened?!"

Hot glances shot toward Max as his voice bounced off the marble walls and ceiling of the expansive room. A pair of know-it-all, teacher-pet types shook their heads disapprovingly before returning to their reading assignments. Max glanced back at his mother, hoping to avoid another "quiet voice" lecture, but she was nowhere in sight.

Great.

Max turned back towards Mr. Gabriel.

"And?"

"And…" Mr. Gabriel paused, before giving a slight shrug of his large shoulders, "The rest is history. Literally. History. The plagues and famines came to an end."

"Wait! You mean just like that—like right on cue?" Max quizzed. "But why? That seems like a bit of a coincidence."

"Well, you might be right, Max. Others thought the same thing. One myth in particular says that a group of men had found the source of this darkness and somehow stopped it."

"A group of medieval men? You mean like knights in armor?"

"No, not so much knights, more like…"

"Monks?" Max offered up.

Gabe turned abruptly towards Max, and cocking his head, peered directly at Max once more. "And how would you know about that?"

Max stiffened at the question, "Well, I mean, it's just a wild guess?" he offered innocently, shrugging his shoulders in response. "It *was* the Middle Ages—monasteries were the thing then, places of learning, right?" Looking to shift the focus away from himself, Max grabbed the remaining empty book boxes sitting behind the display board and stacked them neatly to the side of the table.

"Well, yeah, I suppose." Mr. Gabriel thought for a moment, again stroking his chin. "It's just that it's taken me years of research to uncover that information. But yes, that was the rumor, or mythology, or whatever you want to call it. I think of it as a legend because it has its roots in actual facts."

"What kind of facts?" Max inquired.

"That a group of monks, actual real-life monks, mind you, discovered a passage to the source of these evil forces—an underworld of sorts. The legend states that the creatures there were… well… how do I put it?" Mr. Gabriel put his stubby forefinger to his chin, tapping it lightly.

"Yeah? You can tell me—I can handle it." Max insisted, leaning forward enough to almost trip again.

"I'm sure you can, Max. I'm just saying to keep in mind that this is part myth, part actual history, all interesting stuff, but not what we call 'hard science.'"

"Of course." Max nodded agreeably, as if none of this sounded even remotely believable. "I mean, it's important to know what's fact and what's fiction."

"Exactly!" Mr. Gabriel replied. "I couldn't have stated it better myself. So, without alarming you, let's just say these creatures were supposedly 'sucking' the very life out of people and hoarding it somewhere, some mega chamber or cauldron of sorts. Sounds crazy, right? But a story like that provides insight into the way people thought back then. They had no understanding of how life really worked; they suffered from a lot of ignorance; and this provided an easy way to explain all the tragedies of their time. It helped them to regain a sense of control in their lives. So, while they are not to be taken literally, these myths can be used as lessons and examples of how cultures and societies deal with scary unknowns."

"In other words, a metaphor," Max suggested.

"Precisely! That's an excellent way to explain it." Gabe nodded, flipping open his laptop computer in preparation for his video presentation. His eyes narrowed for a moment, as if checking to see whether Max was okay with the explanation or perhaps holding something back. But if that was the case, Max wasn't about to let on.

"So, in this 'fable,' how did the Benedictine monks find a way to cross over to this other side?"

Gabe gave him a puzzled look. "Huh? Did I say they were Benedictine monks?"

"Didn't you?" Max replied quickly, trying to control his expression. "I mean, how else would I have known?" Max reached over to turn on the set of lights over the display board. "Look! All set!"

"Indeed," Gabe said, muttering to himself. "Been working too hard, I guess…"

"So… the crossing over part?" Max asked as if simply providing a helpful reminder to complete his train of thought.

"Oh, yes, well, no one knows that part of the story—that's the mystery," Gabe said as he plugged in his computer. "Some say it was an incantation or ritualistic chant. Others said it had to do with the timing of planets and the movement of stars. Others simply said it was black magic and that they were possessed by mad spirits. Regardless of how they entered this realm, legend states that the monks were able to somehow stop these entities, and shortly afterward, the plagues and famines and wars came to an end."

"So, what became of the monks?"

"We don't know what happened for sure," Gabe said with a shrug. "The monastery where they lived was sacked by the Huguenots a short time later, all the records were lost, and no one ever saw or heard from the monks again. Whether they just hid out or scattered to other places or just vanished, no one knows for sure. What *is* known is that shortly after that, we entered the Renaissance, a period of great scholastic and artistic achievement."

Dittle-ling! Dittle-ling!

A soft alarm sounded. "Oh my, it's almost time for me to start my talk. You're more than welcome to stay, but you already heard the most interesting parts, Max! I rarely dive in that deep, attention spans being so short these days. I'm glad to see you have such a keen interest."

Max smiled and nodded in agreement. At this point the display table brimmed with colorful book covers and well-organized merchandise, as attendees shuffled in and took their respective places in the neat rows of chairs. Mr. Gabriel politely shook his hand and thanked him, giving him an autographed copy of his book before he left.

Max slung his backpack over his shoulder and made his way out of the main library atrium to a small study area in the back of the library. He passed slowly through a narrow row of cloth-bound reference books that rose high to the rafters. As he sauntered, he thumbed his way through pages of glossy illustrations, maps, and diagrams in Mr. Gabriel's book. The towering bookcases blocked out most of the natural window lighting, creating a twilight pathway to his destination.

The cover of the book featured an artist rendering of one of the creatures, a twisted mashup of arms and legs, set in dark hues of deep blue and green. The embossed image made the creature seem all the more real and believable. Max ran his fingers gently over the surface, feeling each groove, sensing the bumpy texture. His eyes dropped down to the title of the book… *The Myths and Magic of the Middle Ages.*

Max plopped his backpack next to the desk in the small study nook he found available. Sitting in the chair, he pulled out his homework, along with a folder and a separate binder full of notes from last night's research. As he sat looking at the book and gazed at the stack of notes in front of him, he thought of all he read and heard the past in the past twenty-four hours.

How could this possibly be coincidence?

His thoughts drifted back to the old professor in the store and Max worried if he was alright. He thought again about the mysterious messages in the tattered old manuscript and wondered if there was some key, some missing piece that he had overlooked.

It's gotta be there, he thought.

Grabbing a chair, he carefully retrieved the prized text from the inside his backpack, pulling out the printed page he had placed within the book's first pages. He held it closer as if to help absorb its meaning.

"From those who guard the eternal truths,
May our lives protect the souls of man.
We pledge to free the captured past,
And seal our world from those who've strayed."

Stumped, he sat back in his chair, rocking slightly back and forth, mulling the words over in his mind. The air in the small back room felt slightly muggy and stale. He hoisted his backpack on top of the desk, placed both hands on top of it, and gently rested his forehead on top of his hands, as if to clear his thoughts.

Bbbbbbzzzzzzzzzz….

The steady humming of fluorescent lights had a sedating effect. The previous late night was just now catching up. Max let out an unexpected yawn, blinked his eyes momentarily as if to ward off sleep, then slowly closed them in surrender. In the background, he recognized the familiar sounds of the library… the flipping of pages, the clearing of throats, the shuffling of chairs. He let out a deep sigh, as his thoughts drifted from the library to somewhere remote and unfamiliar. In this twilight setting, Max could picture the hideous creatures in Gabe's book, as if lined up in endless rows, eyes bulging as he walked between them.

A doorway, Max mumbled to himself. *There has to be some kind of—*

WHAM! A sound rang out. A book falling?

Max felt the air around him reverberate with a swirl of energy.

"There is no entrance, Max!" a raspy voice whispered. *"The doorway has been sealed. Forget about all this!"*

"What!?" Max recoiled at the mysterious voice. "How do you—"

Another swirl appeared out of the corner of Max's eye. As he turned to look, a hand grasped his arm, shaking him firmly.

"L-l-lemmo go!" Max insisted, pulling away.

"Max! Max!!"

Max sat bolt upright in his chair.

"You're nodding off again!" His mother's face appeared in front of him. Taking his face, she held it firmly in both hands. "What's going on with you? And who were you talking to?"

Max looked past his mom, focusing his eyes, scanning the room for any unusual signs.

"I'm telling you, Max, these late-night projects have got to end!" she scolded. "You are obviously sleep deprived."

"What? I mean, yes, definitely, that's what it is." Max nodded, adjusting himself fully. "You're absolutely right, Mom. Sorry about that!"

Max straightened up in his chair, taking a moment to clear his head. His mother's voice tumbled off into the distance as she urgently detailed the remaining tasks to be completed before he left. But as she spoke, a strange thing happened. Max began to mouth every word she was saying in perfect unison, as if he was repeating something she had just said...

Déjà vu! Like I've heard this before! Max thought.

This means the Boggarts are real, he continued to himself, alarmed at the growing realization. *They're stealing time, splicing in false memories, so it can only mean there's something they don't want me to find out!*

CHAPTER 5

Max excused himself from the book fair, telling his mom that he had an important assignment due with Derek, and due to her concern, he needed to do it right away. It was true, he thought. He *did* have an assignment, and he was all about getting to it sooner.

Max half jogged, half ran, the tree lined streets that extended from the county library well past Derek's house. The shadowy branches waved like outstretched arms in the cool evening breeze, fists of leaves opened and closed like long gnarly fingers. He had forgotten how darkness came so early on a brisk October night. Max zipped his jacket up tightly, and leaning forward, quickened his pace. He was about to round the next to last corner when a light flickered up ahead:

TIME & AGAIN USED BOOKS AND COLLECTIBLES

That's odd, he thought, glancing at the time on his phone, then back at the plate glass window that fronted the family bookstore. Uncle Owen was always out of there by seven o'clock. It was nearly 8 p.m., and the light inside the store was too bright to be the normal security lights. And more importantly, it didn't bounce around.

Keeping his distance, Max crouched behind a long, black SUV parked opposite the store and peered over its wide hood. From this vantage point, he spotted what appeared to be a shadowy outline, moving slowly, methodically across the room, a band of light sweeping from one side to the other as it moved. Still crouched, Max sprinted as best he could to the other side of the street and moved up alongside the storefront window. Cautiously he peered into the window, as he checked the door handle.

Huh? Open? Uncle Owen would never leave it unlocked, Max thought to himself. Maybe it was the cleaners, but they usually came on the last Thursday of the month. *Perhaps the schedule got changed*, he wondered. Turning the knob slowly, Max cracked the door open a few inches, phone flashlight in hand to get a better look.

Nothing.

"Hey, anyone here?" Max yelled in, but there was no answer. Max squeezed in quietly through the door and ventured a few steps farther in. Even odder. A dozen or so books were scattered across the front lobby floor, several lay open, their pages standing on end, some twisted and torn. Then, from behind the counter, the shadowy figure reappeared and slowly rose, its back facing Max.

"Wait! Wait right there... I'm calling the cops!" Max shouted, shining his phone at the figure while fumbling to dial 911.

"Don't do that Max, that's not necessary." With that, the dark outline slowly turned to face Max.

"Professor Gutt?"

"Yes Max, it's me. Oh my, and you're just in time! Was hoping you'd stop by, I really need your help—you're just the person we, I mean, I was hoping to—"

"Wait a minute, what are you doing here, I mean here right now? The store's closed, it's past eight o'clock..."

"Right, right, you're exactly right again, Max, that's what I like about you, Max. It's just that I remembered something else I was looking for here and thought... Well, let me show you—come this way, Max."

With that, the professor motioned wildly with both hands and disappeared down the hallway and into the back room where they had just met the previous day.

"But Professor Gutt, why can't you just tell me..." But it was no use. Exasperated and at a loss to understand, Max made his way down the dimly lit corridor and into the back room.

"Professor? Professor Gutt?"

CRASH!

A towering display of books came smashing to the floor behind Max, blocking his exit from the room.

"So glad you're here to help us, Max!" the eerie voices sounded.

Max whirled back around to address the vibrating chorus.

"Help... *us*? What the..."

There in front of him stood Professor Gutt, a menacing, wide smile creeping across his face, eyes piercing with a hint of a yellow, flame-like glow pulsating in each pupil.

"Now where's the manuscript I gave you?"

"You gave me? Why do you need it, I thought—"

"No questions, Max, just give it back to us." The professor leaned in, moving forward toward Max. Max backed up, one step at a time, until he felt the fallen bookcase behind him.

"Who the heck is *us*? Professor, what's wrong with—?"

"With us? Here's what's wrong with us!"

At that, the professor shook for a second, his body quivering from head to toe, eyes rolling upward, and then, without warning, another Professor Gutt seemed to step out of his body and to his right side, then another, then another.

"That's right, Max, us! And we can do this the easy way, you give us the manuscript—or the hard way." The group of four imposters rose up and started moving toward Max, hands stretched wide.

With no room to back up, Max felt around desperately for anything he could get a hold of. Feeling the heft of a dictionary-sized book, he spun it around and hurled it at the foursome, then another, and another in rapid succession. The figures moved instantly to the left and right, dodging the incoming projectiles, and then lunging at Max. He felt a gripping hand encircle his throat, and two other sets of hands, each holding one of his legs. Max attempted to kick wildly.

"Let me go! Get your hands off me!" But it was no use.

Max could feel the final set of hands grabbing his arms, patting each sleeve and then legs.

"Check his jacket, his pockets, he must have it…" demanded one of the voices. A hand reached out to search the inside lining where the manuscript was neatly tucked away.

"Wait, I think this might be it…"

Max bit down hard on the extended hand.

"AHHHHH!!!" a shout of pain sounded. Why that…"

Max felt himself lifted and weightless as his body went airborne across the room.

"THUD!" The hard surface of the opposite wall crumpled his small frame, his head reeling from the impact. Coughing from the loss of breath, he stood back up, the four attackers moving instantly to regain their hold. Max flipped a table over and hid behind it, grabbing a nearby fire extinguisher. A hand shot around the table, and Max kicked, crawled backwards, and braced as four faces peered over the edge, reaching toward him.

"GGGGUUUUUSSSHHHHHH."

The spray of foam shot directly in the blinking yellow eyes of the attackers.

"AAAHHHH!!" the collective voices sounded again, this time in even more agony. The yellow eyes reappeared again, this time through the blanket of foam, giving them an even ghostlier appearance.

"Give it to us now, or this will not end well!" a voice sneered, regaining a hold on Max's throat. He felt the grip tighten as a second pair joined in. Max could feel a pressure in his eyeballs, the sensation you get when you hold your breath for too long: a slow, rhythmic beating that ebbs and flows, like life itself, strong at first, then gradually weaker until nothing is left. Max managed a final gasp as the room began to lose its color, the taunting voices fading into the background.

"Abi!" a voice boomed loudly.

"Abi in malam rem!"

A bolt of electric blue light suddenly pierced the darkness.

Max felt the death grip release and fresh air rushing back to his lungs. He coughed, staggered to stand upright, and instinctively felt for his throat. There, in front of him, stood an enormous, bearded man, wearing what appeared to be a silver breastplate, silver forearm and leg guards, and brandishing a razor-sharp dagger that glowed white-hot.

"Abi in malam rem!" the voice repeated, but this time in a bold tone no one would question. Max swung back around to face his four attackers, only to see the outlines of their faces contorting in pain.

"Abi in malam rem!" the voice repeated, this time with the dagger held high. What remained of the four frightened faces began to lose form, decomposing like month old pumpkins, until only puddles of thick goo remained. Max stared transfixed at the scene, as the slimy substance slithered between the cracks in the wood floor, then completely vanished from sight. Head still reeling, he paused in astonishment, uncertain of what would come next. Slowly, gradually, he turned back around to face the mammoth warrior, hands and arms raised in defense, wondering if the dagger would now be turned on him.

"Shapeshifters," the bearded man uttered in disgust, returning his sword to its sheath. "You can smell 'em a mile away."

Max plopped to the floor in a complete stupor, unable to move, think, or talk. He had just witnessed what appeared to be multiple copies of a frail professor, demolishing their entire store, attempting to choke him out, and then melting like butter into oblivion. Adding to the madness, this thick bearded rescuer, something resembling a Viking warrior, was now perched on a heaping pile of overturned books—all the while claiming the life-like assailants were some type of mutants.

"My name is Zadkiel," the giant stated in a manner much warmer and gentler than moments before. He reached out his huge right hand as if to make amends. Max recoiled, unsure of anything at this point.

"Surely you know about shapeshifters, Max. They can be very annoying but usually not quite this destructive. C'mon, put it there, Max," Zadkiel said, extending his wide-open palm.

Max slowly, hesitantly, reached out his hand to accept the friendly gesture, but in place of the expected handshake, the giant grasped Max's entire arm and flipped him over his shoulder, then proceeded to walk straight toward the back wall. "I think there's something you should see." But all Max could see was the wall they were about to hit.

Not again! He winced, bracing himself to be crushed…

But the next instant, the wall was gone.

CHAPTER 6

Max opened his eyes and saw… nothing! A black emptiness seemed to engulf him as he felt waves of panic surging inside him. Was he dead? Had he been knocked blind from being thrown against the wall? Or worse yet, from walking through one? He ran his hand over his face to see if he was bleeding but felt nothing but a small, cold bead of sweat across his forehead.

"Help!" he yelled instinctively. "Can someone hear me?"

"Yes, I can hear you," came the muffled laugh, followed by a slow deliberate sigh, "and at probably *half* the volume."

"Kadziel?" Max stammered, still hoping the events of the night had been nothing but a horrific dream.

"Close, Max, it's Zadkiel, and yes, I'm right here."

"But who are—I mean, where is *here*?"

"You're in the Garden of Empyrean. You'll be safe here for now."

Max could see no garden—no flowers, no smells, no anything. "There's nothing here," he said.

"Oh, quite the contrary. This is the most delightful garden you've never seen, but you're still operating in Earth vision. Empyrean is a full three clicks, or seven dimensions, removed from your realm. If you'd like, I can adjust your theta waves so you can perceive what is beyond the range of your senses."

Theta waves! Max quickly searched his memory bank. Sam had helped him research a paper on the subject last year for The Washington County Fair. She sourced one of the key data points, he recalled. *"**Theta waves** generate what's known as **theta rhythm**, a brain pattern that underlies various aspects of cognition and behavior, including learning, memory, and spatial navigation."* Could there be even more to these waves?

"Okay," Max said. "Adjust the—um, you know, just do it."

Suddenly he felt a warm palm on the top of his head, followed by a gentle vibrating sensation. His tensed muscles relaxed as his frantic thoughts slowed to a complete halt. Gradually, light appeared around him, like morning sunlight, seeping around the frame of a kitchen door. The light intensified, splitting into a prism of vivid colors. Each color then broke into even more shades, hues, tints, until there were too many to count. Many of the colors had a fluorescent look to them that Max had never even seen before. In the distance he heard what sounded like a waterfall, but the noise itself had a texture to it. It was as if Max was hearing, seeing, and feeling simultaneously in 3-D. Zadkiel smiled at the bewildered look on Max's face.

"Quite a place, wouldn't you say?"

"What *is* this place?" Max asked.

"Depends on where you're from. The Scots call it the Land of the Leal. Some others call it the Celestial City. But for the most part we go by Empyrean. It's the finest real estate this side of Earth."

"So how did I end up here?" Max asked. "Am I… am I dead?"

"No! You're not dead. Nothing like that. You just happened to get caught in a clean-up job I was working."

"What kind of clean-up job?"

"Shapeshifters. They've been breaching the portal between our worlds and causing all kinds of trouble. But we're working on it. We haven't had this problem for quite some time… well, actually, not since…"

"The Dark Ages?" Max ventured.

"Well… exactly. But we don't want to talk about that. Very messy. Should never have happened. Set mankind back centuries."

Max now noticed lush, colorful trees surrounding him, with fruit that seemed to sparkle in the light.

"They knew you were close to finding a way into their world, Max. And if you succeeded, you could shut down their operation and prevent them from feasting on every lifeform in your world, re-energizing to advance their march here—much like they attempted to do seven hundred Earth years ago. They feed on human energy, the human life force. They always have."

"You're talking about the Boggarts?" Max asked.

"No, no, heavens, no. The Boggarts are bureaucrats. Bean-counters. Paper-shufflers. They require very little *prana*."

"Prana—that means life force, right?" asked Max.

"You're on the right track. It's distilled lifeforce that's edible—or drinkable, it's rather thick…"

"Like a cosmic milkshake?" Max mused, channeling his inner Derrick.

Zadkiel allowed himself a slight smile. "Almost. Anyway, the Boggarts are like bank tellers who handle lots of money but don't get to keep it. They just store the time and ration it out. The biggest users are vampires, wereboars, warlocks, fallen angels, ghouls, imps, and to a lesser degree, hobgoblins, sprites, and pixies. They operate on the negative side of the equation, so to speak, so they consume energy rather than generate it. Whenever they can, they try to infiltrate your world so they can siphon out all the life force they can. Usually, it happens during a daydream or a nightmare. Or if you're unconscious, as in a coma. Even when you're about to sneeze."

Bingo! I knew it! Those suckers! Max thought, reassured that his spidey senses were correct while at the same time disgusted at the notion that life-sucking creatures could be one breath away. A momentary shudder ran through him as Zadkiel continued.

"Are you following, Max?" he asked.

"Yeah, I mean absolutely. It's just that these things are, well… creepy."

"The creepiness you feel is because they tend to operate when you're the most vulnerable or unsuspecting. The shapeshifters go in first and check to make sure the coast is clear. They can take the appearance of any person or animal they want, and the only telltale sign is a yellow flash of light you see in their eyes. Once they give the all-clear signal, then the Boggarts come and steal your time, your life force, your prana. They only steal a few seconds, so as not to alert anyone."

"But exactly how do they steal it?" Max asked.

"Technically they don't steal it, they *take* it."

"Take it?"

"Yes, as in taking your breath away, removing the breath of life itself. They twist their heads sideways, open their mouths wide, and inhale. It creates a slight suction effect. Perhaps you've noticed yourself 'catching' your breath or fighting the urge to yawn."

Max wrinkled his brow, disturbed at the very thought of the image. "Then what?"

"Then they blow this prana, this stolen life force, through a small tube into time-tight containers they carry with them called Extractors."

"Couldn't they just zap you with the Extractor?"

"Yes, but you would most definitely feel it." Zadkiel replied. "They want to remain undetected."

"And from there?"

"From there, they bring it back to unload in a central holding system, a time vault so to speak. A few seconds here and there, every single day, from over seven billion people, adds up to a lot of time. We think they've stored over 500 billion years of time. If they store up enough time, more than the collective lifetimes of everyone living today, it will tip the balance in their favor."

"Then what?" Max asked.

"They'll transform, become 'real' as it were, and invade your world. That would make the Dark Ages look like a church picnic. Once in your realm, they would be able to siphon fifty years off a person just by the touch of a hand! Their power would continue to grow exponentially. They crave eternal human form, and the only thing more infinite is their desire for more. They've always had enough energy to enter dreams— what you call nightmares. But recently, as the time vault reaches full capacity, they've begun to physically materialize in small numbers, as you've just witnessed. As we speak, they're preparing to materialize in force, and that must not happen."

Zadkiel paused to allow Max time to fully absorb the information. "I realize this is a lot," he continued, then added, "and there's more. We have reason to believe the Time Vault is seven levels down from here, most likely in… Nemesis."

"Nemesis?" Max said, recalling the familiar word.

"It's the equivalent of a basement or parking garage in one of your buildings. Imagine we're on the seventh floor. From here you could go down all the way to the main lobby. On the way down you would pass floors, we call them realms, of angels, patron saints, then good fairies and a few wise wizards. Then there are the sublevels that go deep underground. Nemesis is the bottom floor. And it's guarded by Abaddon, a dark soul if there ever was one. He is the keeper of the void, the ruler of that realm."

"So… why don't you just go down there and stop this guy?"

"Against regulations," Zadkiel replied with a grim look. "I can only go down to the main level—that's your level, Earth. Actually, both sides can enter Earth. It's the only place where both energies overlap, positive and negative, which is why there's so much conflict. But for me, the world below is forbidden. However, Max, there is someone who can enter it."

"Like… some kind of super-angel? An archangel?"

"No, Max. Actually, someone who resides in the center, the neutral zone. Someone who can transcend both realms. Someone like you."

"Me! Are you kidding? In some dungeon of doom?" The idea was so preposterous that it was all Max could do not to laugh. "No way! I'd last all of five seconds."

"Well, that all depends, Max. Their 'world' isn't all what it appears to be. It's important to keep that in mind whenever you feel the need for help. For that you'll need both insight and vision, a third eye of sorts."

"What third eye? I know nothing about—"

"It's right here," Zadkiel reassured him, tapping gently three times on Max's forehead. In an instant Max saw what appeared to be a brilliant, egg-shaped object floating in front of him, bejeweled from top to bottom, light beaming from what looked like a glowing emerald, in its otherwise hollow core. Max marveled at its ornate beauty, and as he observed, it slowly began turning, revealing a string of mysterious lettering wrapped around its outer edges.

"It's written in Empyrean, Max, don't worry about it."

"What's it for?" Max asked in astonishment, mesmerized by the sparkling, luminous glow. Curious, he reached out to touch it. The textured stone felt solid and weighty in his hand, and as he squeezed it, small blue waves of what looked like miniature lightning spread up his outstretched arm, along his shoulder and up his neck until it reached the crown of his head.

"Let's just say it's part of a bigger story—one you'll understand more the further you go—just as your father did," Zadkiel replied.

"Wait!" Max said, almost dropping the stone. "My fa–? What do *you* know about—?"

"What I need to know, Max, and now it's your time to go."

"But where am I going?"

"That's something only you can decide, Max."

"Hold on. You don't mean that Nemesis place! 'Cause that ain't happening, okay? I'm supposed to be home right now." Max felt his entire body begin to stiffen, his mind racing at the very thought. "I've got work and tests… a life… This is crazy. I must be having a fever dream!" As fear flooded his mind, the garden around him began to fade from sight.

"You can do it, Max! I have complete confidence in you. Just look for the way. The balance must be restored. I'll help you any way I can, but whatever you do, avoid Abaddon…" Zadkiel's voice began fading, and then all turned black again.

CHAPTER 7

"**S**on, are you all right?" A bright flashlight shone directly into Max's eyes, obscuring the identity of his interrogator.

"Yeah… I think so," he said, slowly pushing books off his legs.

"That was a brave thing you did, running in here during a burglary. But it wasn't a smart thing."

Max could now see the face of a police officer, one of several now scouring the store, flashlights pointing in every direction in search of clues. Max now found himself back in the family bookstore. Or what was left of it.

"I didn't do this, officer," Max offered apologetically.

"I know, son, your backpack had your name and number, and we called the owner, your Uncle Owen, correct? He and your mother on their way right now." It was only a matter of seconds before Max heard the screeching of tires and the concerned voices of both his mother and uncle as they made their way frantically through the front lobby, then the long hallway, the sound of broken glass announcing each step.

"Max! Honey!" his mother cried, worry etched onto her face. "Are you all right? I thought you were at Derek's! What happened?"

The officer answered, to Max's eternal relief. After all, he thought, what could he have told her?

"We think he stumbled on a burglary in progress, ma'am. He took quite a bump to the head. We found him right here, groggy and a bit incoherent. Probably from the blow." Then, turning to Max, the officer said, "If you're feeling up to it, son, could you tell us what you saw? Anything at all might help."

What I saw! thought Max to himself. *First of all, I saw four mutant copies of a mad professor melt like the inside of a grilled cheese sandwich into the floor. Then I saw some archangel and a fluorescent garden. Forget the bump on the head! If I tell them all that, they'll think I've suffered brain damage.* He bought some time by rubbing the lump on his head and slowly twisting his neck, first in a circle, then side to side.

"Well, I saw a light on in the back room, and when I went to investigate, these, well, thugs were throwing things around and smashing up the place. After that I'm not sure what exactly happened." As he answered he looked cautiously at his mom and uncle, searching for the slightest hint of yellow flashes in their eyes—unsure he could trust anyone or anything at this point.

"Could be gang or drug-related," the officer said matter-of-factly. "There's been a string of robberies in the area." Turning, he yelled back to his partner, "Hey, Smitty!" And to one of the other cops across the room, he shouted, "Check the cash register and get with Mr..." He turned to Max's uncle.

"Peters," Uncle Owen responded. "Owen Peters."

"Get with Mr. Peters to see if any money is missing. We'll also need to dust for fingerprints." He looked back at Max. "We'll be in touch later to get a full written statement. But for now, you should probably have that bump looked at."

Max shook his head. "No. I'm fine. I've had worse. I really just want to go home right now."

"Well, of course you do!" his mother said as Uncle Owen helped him to his feet. "We'll have to get some ice for that nasty bump…"

"But what about the store, this mess?" Max objected.

"We can take care of that later," his uncle said with a look of concern. "For now, it's bed rest. No ifs, ands or buts!"

During the drive home, Max could hear his mother and Uncle Owen talking in hushed tones, the kind they used when adults are worried but act as though nothing is wrong. His only thought was the manuscript.

The manuscript!

He double checked his inside pocket, feeling around desperately for the worn leather binding.

Ah ha! Safe!

Max breathed a sigh of relief. At least he had held on, they didn't get the manuscript. But if they knew he had it, what else were they looking for? And where was the *real* professor?

* * *

Once home, Max's mom insisted he plant himself in one of the yellow flowered, vinyl-covered kitchen chairs, while she attended to his head wound, starting with a thorough rinse, an application of iodine, and a cold compress.

"What to do with you, Max," she said, shaking her head slowly back and forth. "Why wouldn't you just call someone? What would your father have said? You just about scared your Uncle Owen and me to death getting that call from the police."

The room grew silent. *Exactly! What would he say?* A tumble of thoughts poured through Max's mind. *Theta waves. Empyrean. Nemesis.* Max concentrated as if to somehow shift his focus to another realm, somewhere distant and exotic, somewhere where things flowered and glowed, but more importantly, where things somehow made more sense. But all he could hear was the low hum of the refrigerator and the crackle of the cold plastic seat beneath as he moved around.

As her work neared completion, Max hesitated for a moment, before breaking the silence.

"Mom?" Max inquired quietly as she finished dressing the wound.

"Yeah, honey?" she replied, still intent on her duties.

"What do you think *really* happened to Dad?"

"What exactly do you mean?" she replied, stiffening for a moment, as if caught off guard by the comment. She snipped a final piece of white first aid tape and, parting his thick hair, pressed it firmly on his scalp.

"I mean, do you believe all that bull crap about what they say happened? The explosion and all? It doesn't add up."

His mother stopped, and holding her breath for a brief moment, turned slowly to address Max, squaring his shoulders to look him squarely in the eyes.

"Why are you asking this right now, honey?" she asked. "You know what happened. Your father was involved in highly sensitive work, risky work, and sometimes things happen, things that we don't always understand."

"But what's the chance they never found any trace of him? I mean, do you ever wonder if he, if he just left?"

"Left?" she repeated, her eyes beginning to moisten with emotion. "Why Max, why would you ever—your father…"

"My father what?" Max replied, meeting her gaze with equal intensity. "He left a long time ago, way before the accident. And maybe that's what he wanted, maybe he left because he loved what he was doing. Maybe he loved it more than us."

"That's not true, Max, and that's not fair," she insisted, sitting upright. "Your father worshiped you. You're the very reason he did the work he was doing. He was trying to do what's best for you, for all of us. And sometimes that requires choices, difficult ones."

Max fell silent. He knew the facts about what had happened, but facts have no feelings.

"Did dad ever mention working with a professor?"

"What do you mean? Your dad worked with all sorts of professors. Max, where are all these questions coming from?"

"I ran into someone at the bookstore, a professor named Guttenburg. Uncle Owen said he had mentioned something about working at ETH Zurich. Maybe he knew Dad."

"Well, who's to say, honey, that's a big place," his mom replied tenderly. "Here's what I think. I think seeing your father's bookstore torn apart, knowing how much you two spent time there, has you understandably upset. For now, why don't you give yourself permission to just relax and rest up; that was quite the time you just had this evening."

Quite the time, indeed, Max thought.

* * *

"Maybe you were just hallucinating," Derek ventured. "After all, you took a pretty good knock to your gourd. I got hit like that in hockey once, remember? Took a puck right to the forehead. Saw all kinds of weird stuff. But anyway, I would have given anything to have been there tonight, Max, I would have—"

"Trust me, Derek, you would not have wanted to be there, and this was no hallucination," Max replied, as he adjusted the lighting on his laptop camera, the video call glitching for a moment as they spoke. Max adjusted the volume as well, so as to not alert his mother that he was back working on his computer, not resting in bed. "And before you even ask, *no*, I didn't eat any funny mushrooms."

"Okay, then how do you explain it?" Derek replied.

"I can't," Max said thinking aloud, tapping an unsharpened pencil on top of his laptop. "But I think I know someone who can…"

"Who?" Derek quizzed.

"Sam."

"Sam? Why would she know anything about getting pummeled in the head."

"Because she worked with that VolunTeen program last semester, the one over at Miriam Hospital."

"So?"

"So, she worked with patients who had been in comas, some of them for weeks or months. She got to speak to some of them, right after they woke up, and I remember her saying they talked about the same stuff, visiting other realms, seeing lights, hearing things. Maybe—"

"Yes, exactly, Max, *hearing things*. You were just hearing things."

"Never mind, just patch her in," Max insisted.

"Alright," Derek replied, shaking his head as he shot off an invite. The screen blinked for a second or two, a phone ring murmured momentarily in the background, before a familiar face popped up."

"What's up, guys?" Sam chirped brightly.

"Wait till you hear this, Sam," Derek prefaced. "You thought the last story was strange."

"Okay, hit me, I'm all ears," she said, taking a sip from what remained of a green smoothie.

Max detailed the events of the evening, starting with his visit with Mr. Gabriel, making sure to include as much detail as possible. "And so, what do you think?"

"Well," Sam replied, weighing her response thoughtfully, unsure what exactly to make of it. "Regardless of what happened, I'm just glad you're alright."

"Yeah, I was going to say the same thing, Max, glad they didn't off you," Derek echoed quickly, embarrassed he hadn't said something earlier.

"Great, thanks, I made it. So what are you thinking, Sam?" Max insisted.

"Well, it could be a number of things based on what you're describing."

"Well, we've already ruled out mushrooms," said Derek, "so what's left?"

"I think it could have something to do with the trauma itself, the shock from all that, something dissociative," she replied.

"Dissociative? You mean like a fugue state? Something psychogenic?" Max proposed.

"Exactly," Sam agreed, with a definite nod.

"English, please?" Derek interjected.

"It's a temporary condition where a person experiences memory loss, sort of like amnesia, and ends up in some unexpected place, real or imagined," Sam explained. "It's how the mind handles super stressful events, which is most likely what happened."

"Let me guess," Derek replied, "you read a book about all this."

"Three actually, if you're keeping count," Sam said, nodding proudly.

"I get it, I mean that obviously makes more sense," Max replied, "but there was something more to this, something felt very real. I know it sounds like any crazy person who hears and sees things, but this *is* different."

"Different how?" asked Derek.

"Well, like how this Zadkiel knew about Nemesis, and about the vault…" Max stated.

"Maybe you were just remembering what the professor told you, so you dreamed it up as part of your frog state, or whatever it is that you two seem to know so much about."

"Fugue state," both Max and Sam in unison.

"But Derek *does* have a point, Max," Sam injected, sympathetically. "You had just heard all these things from the professor and could have incorporated them into what happened; it's your brain trying to protect you, Max, that's all."

Dejected, Max slid down lower in his seat, mulling over their opinions, the bump on his head pulsated slightly. "I did take a bit of a beat down, didn't I?"

"Yeah!" they both agreed, giving Max a nod while eyeing each other with a supportive glance.

Max let out a sigh.

"But then these 'people' I saw, these melting creatures, so you're suggesting those were part of the dream, too? Because I have some pretty hard evidence right here on my head," he said pointing to the freshly taped gauze.

"No! Of course not," Sam countered. "You got jumped for sure, but who knows who they were. Your uncle told you to rest up, right? That's probably the best thing for now. Maybe you'll see things more clearly in the morning."

"Wait! What did you just say, Sam?" Max demanded.

"She said to sleep it off, Max," Derek repeated.

"No, Sam, you said I need to see things more clearly," Max insisted.

"Yes?" Sam said hesitantly. "And…?"

"That's what Zadkiel said too, that I needed to see things clearly, and he gave me some kind of jeweled stone with a shining eye in it. He said I would need it."

"Like some kind of treasure? Some heirloom? Maybe there's a reward for it. You didn't mention that, let's see it!" Derek said excitedly.

"That's just it, I don't have it. I must have dropped it when I came to. It must still be back at the bookstore, under the pile of books and chairs. We've got to go back."

Sam and Derek eyed each other for a moment.

"Listen, Max, if this will make you feel better I'm all about it, but you gotta admit, it just sounds a little out there—just being real," Derek stated. "Plus, I really wanna see what they did to the place. Creepers."

"Same here," Sam agreed. "Let's get it cleaned up tomorrow and maybe we'll find some clues as to what exactly they were after."

That's just it, Max thought to himself, *I* know *what they were after.*

Chapter 8

WWWWAAAAAAHHHHH!

The sharp pitch of the shop vac sounded loudly, sucking up various pieces of torn paper, broken glass, and the dried remnants of the fire extinguisher foam. Max suctioned each piece up slowly, inspecting them one by one, looking for any evidence of the prized object.

"Hey! Max! Maybe it would be easier to just hunt down the old professor," Derek shouted over the din of the vacuum, biting the end off a protein bar. "He's got to know more than he's letting on, assuming he's not, you know…" Derek motioned, making a slicing move across his throat.

Max stopped, turned off the machine, and looked up at Derek, perched on top of a wooden half shelf.

"Really? Why do you *always* have to go there, Derek?" Max objected, kneeling over and to pick up a handful of the scattered books strewn across the dark oak flooring, then handing them gently to Sam. The torn ones she placed in a large black plastic bag, while the remainder she stacked neatly in cardboard boxes.

"You know another option?" Sam suggested, eyeing Derek. "You could actually help by sorting through some of this mess and taking out this trash." She held up the heavy, nearly full trash bag, and motioned for Derek to come grab it.

The trio had met right after school. Uncle Owen had gladly accepted their offer, equipping them with cleaners, wipes, brooms and bags while he filled out additional police paperwork, installed new locks, and filed the insurance claim.

"Hmmm…" Max murmured, grabbing up the last remaining books piled in front of a set of built in bookcases.

"I'm not seeing anything that looks like some crown jewel." Derek said in exasperation. He grabbed another trash bag and dragged it next to several others, stacking them by a rear exit door.

"So this thing you remember getting, was it like an amulet?" Sam asked, puzzled still.

"Sort of, this Zadkiel told me it was part of a bigger story," Max replied.

"So more of a talisman, something with some special kind of power?" Sam asked, trying to picture just what Max was looking for.

"Do you always have to talk like a dictionary?" Derek complained.

"No, she's right, Zadkiel said it was like a third eye."

"Third eye?" Derek repeated, puzzled.

"A lot of cultures believe in the third eye, a kind of intuition, the ability to see beyond normal sight," Sam continued.

"Well, all I see is this empty bookcase wall in front of you," Derek complained. "We've cleaned everything else out."

"Wait!" Max interrupted. "That's it!"

"What's it?" they both chimed in at once.

"The third eye, it's about seeing beyond what's physically in front of you," Max said, feeling the smooth wooden backing on the bookshelves in front of him. "This is the same wall that Zadkiel walked through—it's some sort of clue, to go beyond the wall."

"But how?" Derek questioned. "Smash our way through it?"

"No," Max insisted. "I remember as a kid working with my dad back here. And there used to be a big broom closet, right about where this bookcase is now."

"So what happened to it?" Sam inquired, interested to know just where Max was going with his line of reasoning.

"I don't know, I haven't thought much of it, I was pretty young, but now I'm wondering…"

Max was now actively standing on the bottom shelves, running his hands across the upper ones, inspecting the ceiling above.

"What are you—" Derek began to ask.

"Dad had a collection of rare artifacts, ones that were part of his research project. He showed me a few of them, stuff from the Middle Ages, medallions, old crosses, totems, that sort of stuff."

"And…" Derek inquired, "your point?"

"When Dad went missing, we had a memorial service, you remember, Derek? And when I looked through some of his awards and memorabilia, I realized the artifacts were missing. I assumed he had stored them somewhere."

"Like a secret room?" Sam said, nodding her head with a growing sense of excitement.

"Yeah! Dad used to tell me 'Whenever I'm gone, in case of emergency, go to the bookstore.' Maybe he literally meant when he was gone, in case he went missing."

"But then what does that have to do with 'in case of emergency' and 'go to this bookstore'?" Derek asked, now pulling up alongside Max, as if to understand what he was looking for.

"Maybe he was being literal, IN CASE OF EMERGENCY," Max stated emphatically, pointing to a red fire alarm box with those exact same words on it located next to the bookcase. "Let's see if it's what I think it is."

"Wait! Max don't pull the—"

Max flipped open the protective glass cover on the alarm and pulled the lever with a swift, hard motion. Derek winced in anticipation of a screaming alarm. Sam likewise took a step back.

Nothing.

"Huh!" Derek offered. "Well, so much for fire safety, it doesn't even work."

Ccccrrrreeeaaaaakkkkkkk.

Just as Derek spoke, a rumbling noise sounded. Then the entire bookcase shuddered momentarily, before slowly opening, second by second, inch by inch, until it stood perpendicular to the wall, with an opening appearing on each side.

"What the…?" Derek exclaimed, mouth gaping open.

The room around them filled with a thin puff of dusty air that gushed out from behind the bookcase opening.

"There!" Sam exclaimed, pointing into the dark openings. "I think there's something on the other side, some kind of room."

Instinctively the three of them flipped open their cell phones, lights on, huddling tightly together to gain a better look inside.

"It's where the old broom closet was for sure," Max announced. "But it's full of… Huh? It looks like…" Max shone his light around to get a better look.

"Dude, what is this place?" Derek exclaimed.

"It looks like my dad's old office. I recognize some of these things in here. C'mon, let's take a look," he beckoned, motioning them in.

The trio slowly made their way through the narrow passage openings on each side of the bookcase. Their lights now lit upon an odd assortment of items, a faded yellow globe stitched together with thin curled strips of leather, an antique spyglass crafted from mahogany and polished brass, a collection of what looked like medieval swords in hammered metal sheaths. A roll top writing desk stood front and center between two tall bookshelves, filled with what appeared to be equally aged books on mathematics, geography, philosophy, and art. On the top of the shelves stood the outlines of figurines, their eyes peering at the three in the dim light.

"Wait! Those look like the same creatures Mr. Gabe showed me!" Max said in amazement.

"Mr. Who?" Derek asked.

"The author, the guest speaker at Mom's book fair, he had a set that looked identical to these," Max pulled them down and began inspecting them closely.

"But why would your dad's stuff be here, Max?" Sam questioned. "I thought he worked from home when he was in town."

"He did," Max insisted, "until a couple years ago. He had an office in the basement, with a safe, where he said he kept valuables."

"And?" she continued.

"He said some of these things, some work-related stuff, were too valuable to keep there, so he moved them out. I figured he took them with him to Zurich when he left on sabbatical, or he put them in storage, but it looks like they're all here," Max said in amazement, turning slowly around again, almost losing his balance.

"Yeah, what is the deal with Zurich?" Sam asked, now sitting in the one office chair, spinning slightly side to side on its swivel, as if testing it out. "Super weird coincidence, him *and* the professor? Didn't you say your father worked on some heavy-duty research program there?"

"Yeah, he was working on a project called SCION," Max said. "I don't know a whole lot about it, other than it involved the university and a few different government agencies—not sure exactly which ones. It was always pretty hush hush, that's how these things are at that level."

"That's it? Just some mysterious SCION thing, like some spy novel? Did it stand for anything?" Derek asked, a bit perplexed.

"Sure, are you ready for this?" Max replied before taking a big breath. "Scalability, Control, and Isolation on Next-Generation Networks. How's that for a mouthful?"

"Wait? Isn't that that 'next internet' thing, like internet 3.0?" Sam asked.

"Sort of," Max replied, now pulling out each book on the shelf and looking behind them. "It was supposed to be a way to connect more securely and to keep the bad guys from hacking into things."

"And your dad was part of it?" Sam asked.

"He was studying how the entire internet could operate on invisible energy lines—'path aware networking,' he called it—it was all very experimental."

"Path aware networking?" Derek shook his head. "Sounds more like a hiking club to me."

"Regardless, it never happened." Max shook his head. "Whatever the research was, the fire in the data center destroyed everything, the computer lab, the equipment, the notes. There was nothing left."

"First, an accident where your father worked, second, a break-in at the bookstore he owned—it's like there's nowhere to hide," Derek said glumly.

"That's just it," Max said, now opening up various books and looking inside each one. "I think Dad *was* looking for somewhere to hide—somewhere to hide a clue about what he was working on. Someone or something wanted to get their hands on it. I think that's why he moved everything out of the house and into here."

"Are you kids about finished back there?" came the loud shout from Uncle Owen. "I can come back and help now; in fact, I'll bring an extra broom with me." Footsteps sounded down the hallway.

"No!!" Max yelled. "I mean no, that's okay, Uncle Owen! We got this, we'll be right up, we're—we're just bagging up the trash."

Max spun back around to Derek and Sam, "Quick, let's get out of here,"

The threesome bolted out of the small hidden room, Max and Derek each pushing the large bookcase back around until it clicked into place.

SNAP!

"Hey!" Uncle Owen popped in unexpectedly. "I said I could help you with… wait! What exactly have you three been up to?" he said with a look of suspicion.

"Up to?" Max replied. "We were just—"

"Just working yourselves to the bone, that's what," Uncle Owen interrupted. "This looks like nothing ever happened back here, great job, all of you," he said with a satisfied smile. "Drag those three bags there to the big dumpster out back and meet me out front. I owe you all pizza," he said as he headed back down the hallway, whistling along as he made his way to the front lobby.

"Wow, that was close," Derek exhaled.

"Yeah, agreed," Max said. "I don't think we should tell anyone about this, not right now. I don't want to get anyone else involved until we figure out what's going on, so for now, let's keep this secret a secret," he said, looking especially hard at Derek.

"What, me? Why are you looking at me? I say we all swear on it, spit swear," he said, wetting the palm of his hand.

"Ewwww!" said Sam. "Gross! How about we just agree not to say anything?" Sam offered.

"Okay then," Derek conceded, and as if for emphasis added, "like our lives depend on it."

That's just it, Max thought to himself. *They just might.*

CHAPTER 9

"**S**orry for doubting you, Max," Derek offered up on the way home. The three were seated in the back of Uncle Owen's wagon, while he drove with earbuds in, humming to himself along the way. "The whole dream thing sounded so whack, but whoever this Zadkiel guy is, he obviously has some inside information. I still don't get it, that whole thing with the wall, your dad's office, but something is definitely up. Even if it was just a vision or hologram or something, it's coming from somewhere."

"That's alright, Derek," Max said reassuring him, "I would have thought the same thing."

"Hey, I have an idea!" Sam offered up.

"What's that?" Max replied.

"There's a career day at the hospital tomorrow, sort of an open house, where you can find out about different medical specialties. You guys could come, and I'll show you the ward where I volunteer. Maybe then you could talk to one of the doctors there about these… trance states, these in-between worlds, see what they might know."

"You can say it, Sam," Derek replied.

"Okay, fugue states, yes, they might have some insights into what's happening."

"That's a great idea," Max replied. "It certainly can't hurt, and maybe we'll find out just where these messages are coming from, the mind or somewhere beyond."

Uncle Owen dropped off Sam at her dad's upstairs loft apartment, thanked her for all her help, and returned the boys home. They agreed to meet up at the hospital immediately after school the next day, right after Derek's soccer practice.

* * *

The double sliding doors opened briskly as Max and Derek entered LifeSpan, the long-term care wing at The Miriam Hospital. Sam was there to greet them, sign them in, and provide name badges.

"Here, it's right his way," she said, taking them down a maze of hallways and nurses' stations. There was a whirl of activity in every direction: dinner trays rattling on metal serving carts, glistening polished floors bouncing with bright fluorescent light.

"Max, Derek, I want to introduce you to Dr. Metcalf, he's the head of the department here, and a board-certified neurologist."

"Glad to meet you, Dr. Metcalf," Max said with a firm shake of the hand. Derek stood slightly off, behind Max's left shoulder, nodding his head in acknowledgement.

"Nice to meet the both of you," Dr. Metcalf said, with a broad smile. "I hear you're interested in what we do here?"

"Yes, we're sort of researching just what happens to people when they regain consciousness."

"Great question, Max," Dr. Metcalf stated. "And it's an evolving field of study for us as well. We learn something new each day. What we know for now is that these patients experience something few of us will ever know."

"What's that?" Derek offered up, almost surprised at his own question.

"The mind turning off, shutting down, going inward and silent."

"But what does that mean?" Max pressed, his curiosity piqued by the statement.

"Well, that's just it, the person is still alive, living, breathing, but not necessarily thinking, not in the traditional everyday sense. They are aware, but just on a different level, an internal one. That's why it's often hard for them to explain and articulate their experience when they wake up. For all we know it might not even be an experience."

"Then what exactly would it be?" Sam inquired, equally as intrigued.

"More of a dimensional shift, another frequency so to speak, one that we don't normally operate on, like a different channel on the tv or radio. There's a lot to be studied and this is just what some people theorize. But I'm glad you all have taken such a keen interest. And I encourage you to keep up your studies. We could use some bright minds in this field."

With that, Dr. Metcalf excused himself and made his way down the hall to complete his visitations.

"Interesting," Max nodded. "Another dimension, a different frequency... like theta waves."

"Like what?" Derek asked.

"Oh, nothing, just thinking aloud," Max said looking off to a row of beds in a large, dimly lit room. "Sam, what's in here?"

"That's where our long-term patients stay, the ones that are still in a deep coma state. We try to keep it as dark and quiet as possible so as not to disturb them. I can take you in there as long as we are masked up."

The three entered the room, the soft hum of ventilators humming in the background. Max looked at various patients in what appeared to be deep sleep, their chests rising and falling, as if in some coordinated rhythm.

"Maa. Maa... Max..." came a hoarse whispered voice.

"What? Did you say something to me, Sam?" Max asked.

"No! No, I didn't... I think it came from over there." Sam pointed to the far side of the room,

"B-b-be, careful, Max..." the voice continued, trailing off.

The three drew nearer to get a look at just where the voice was coming from. A thin, white sheet covered most of the figure, a receding white hairline revealed a face hidden beneath an oxygen mask.

"Professor Gutt!" Max exclaimed in disbelief.

"What?" Derek said in a muffled half-shout. "This is the guy you were telling us about?"

"Here," Sam rushed in, offering to help remove the mask as he struggled to speak. As she did so, she pushed a button to alert the medical teams. "Don't worry, we'll have some help here in just a minute," she said reassuring him. "Max, help get him comfortable."

Max helped prop the professor's head up a bit, rearranging the pillow behind his neck, allowing him to clear his throat.

"*He's there, Max,*" he said with an air of urgency, struggling with each word.

"Who's there?" Max repeated, looking directly into the professor's intent stare.

"Your father!" he said. "I should have told you."

"My father? He's where… in Zurich?"

"No Max, in Nemesis…" came the reply. "I know he is… there's no other explanation."

"Wait! You knew him, but how?"

"Yes, we worked together on a very special project, and he was making great progress."

"You mean SCION?"

"Yes, he found new pathways, ways to connect without wires, without satellites, based solely on energy waves." Professor Gutt stopped for a minute, coughed repeatedly, and held a finger to his throat, as if begging for a moment to regain his voice.

"Here," Sam insisted, pouring a cup of water and holding it up to his lips. "Just take a minute, you don't need to—"

"It's okay," he said, taking a deep breath. "Max, it was your father who realized the only thing keeping the system from working was a leak." He gulped as if to take in more air.

"A leak?" Max asked, unsure if he should be encouraging the professor to keep speaking but needing to know more. "What kind of leak?"

"Dark energy," the professor stated, "something was absorbing the energy needed to power the program, and your father said he had identified the source. That's when the accident happened, the night he went to test his theory."

Max could hear the shuffle of hurried feet coming down the hallway. The head nurse turned into the far end of the long room and began walking directly toward them.

"Here, clear out, we've got this!" she shouted from a distance, waving an attendant along with her.

"They thought I still had the manuscript," the professor chuckled. "I knew about your father's secret back room. He used the manuscript for his calculations, to find his way in, but they were looking for one more missing piece. And I knew they would come back looking for it."

"Here, step back, clear out," came the directive as the nurse quickly approached.

With that, the Professor handed Max his cane.

"Use it, Max. Just find a way in. Your father relied on his mind, but his work and his lab are now gone. You must find another path, using a different kind of instrument," the Professor said, and with that he reached out and tapped Max gently on the chest.

ZZZZZZZZZZZZZZZZZZZZZZZZZZZZZ.

"He's gone back under," the head nurse muttered tersely, now shoving Max to the side and shining a lighted pen to look into the Professor's eyes. The stare looked blank and empty.

"Did he say anything?" she said, looking at the three of them.

"Yes," Sam replied. "He said a few sentences, he spoke to Max."

"I'm sure nothing that made sense," the nurse replied, as if to confirm her own thoughts. Then turning, she gave Sam a quick nod. "Thank you for your help and for letting us know, we've got it from here."

With that the trio was ushered out of the dark room. Standing back out in the bright lights of the central nursing station, Max stood, shaking his head.

"What are you thinking, Max?" Derek demanded. "What should we do now?"

"Yeah," Sam asked, equally concerned with the expression on Max's face.

"I'm going to do what the professor said," Max stated, his gaze fixed. "I need answers, and I'm going to find a way in."

"A way in to where?" Derek insisted.

"Where else?" Max replied.

Nemesis.

59

CHAPTER 10

"Coffee?"

"Uh, no thanks, ma'am," Max replied.

"And you?"

"Yes, a double espresso," Derek eagerly nodded.

"You need that like a hole in the head," Sam said, nursing a hot green tea.

The three had gathered in a small, red leather booth in the coffee shop in the front lobby of the hospital. Out of the window that faced the street, a van pulled up reading SMELL THE ROSES; a hurried driver unloaded bouquets of flowers while avoiding a lady walking her three robust-looking basset hounds.

"So?" Derek asked, sipping the steaming cup of froth, burning his lip slightly on the first attempt.

"So... what?" Max replied somewhat distracted, as he carefully examined the carved wooden cane the professor had given him.

"So how are we going to break into this Nemesis place? Assuming, of course, the professor's right."

Sam nodded in agreement.

"What do you mean *we?*" Max asked, pivoting back to stare at both of them.

"I mean like you, me, and Sam," Derek replied matter-of-factly.

"I know what 'we' means, Derek," Max said in a voice of exasperation, "but this is my fight, I don't want to involve you two any further—"

"Listen, Max," Sam insisted, "Derek and I both know you, you're stubborn, and you're not going to let go of this. If your dad is involved, you're going to keep digging, and it's going to lead to more trouble. Just look at what's happened already to both you and the professor. Besides, from what we've seen the past couple days, we know too much."

60

"That's just it, I never meant to—"

"I know," Sam replied. "So, let's figure it out."

The booth fell silent. Derek and Sam sat quietly, eyes fixed on Max, waiting in anticipation for his response.

"Okay," Max finally admitted. "You're right. We need to stick together. It's not like we can go to the police with any of this; it would make no sense."

"So, back to this Nemesis place," Derek asked, "just how do we find it? It's not like we have a map."

"That's just it, it might not be a place," Max said.

"Then what would it be?" Sam questioned.

"Perhaps a dimension, an energy field of some sort. The professor said my dad was working on an idea, a theory, based on the manuscript."

With that, Max took a cautious look around before pulling the tattered book from his backpack, laying it open on the table.

"I knew I recognized the handwriting," he said, poring over the pages. "He must have been searching through old texts for clues to how previous generations dealt with dark energy, so the medieval times would make sense. There must be something he realized in this script; he must have known about the monks."

As he thought, Max kept tapping the cane he held in his left hand, as if keeping time with his thoughts.

Ka-thunk! Ka-thunk!

"That's odd," Max said, sitting back up straight in his seat.

"What?" asked Derek. "The handwriting? The drawings?"

"No," Max stated, "this." And with that, he tapped the cane forcibly up and down, striking the surface of the floor with twice the force. "Did you hear that?"

"Yes, I heard something, sounded almost like a rattle," Sam replied.

"Huh?" Max picked up the cane and held it closer to his ear, shaking it a couple more times. "Seems to be coming from here in the handle, the top of the cane."

Max grabbed the carved head of the cane, formed in the shape of a dragon's head, and gave it a hard twist.

Pop!

"What's that?!" Derek asked, as the top of the cane separated, revealing a small cavity the size of an egg. Tucked inside of it was a tightly wrapped object, bundled in a fuzzy felt material.

"I'm not quite sure," Max replied, carefully laying the item down in the center of the table in front of them. Around the edges of the cloth, a faint glow could be seen, pulsing gently. Max took the edges of the cloth and unwrapped the mystery package.

"Holy crap!" Derek exclaimed.

"Zadkiel's stone!" Sam gasped, eyes wide open.

"Okay, for sure it wasn't just a vision, Max—this thing is for real!" Derek exclaimed, breathless from more than just the coffee.

Max sat for a moment, dumbfounded, staring at the object he now held in his hands. It felt just as he remembered, weighty, textured, and slightly warm to the touch.

"The professor must have removed it from your dad's study when he first came to get the manuscript," Sam said, mesmerized by the sight of the bejeweled stone.

"Yeah," Max agreed, peering at the center of the glowing ember-like jewel. "That's why those changelings came back to the bookstore. They wanted the manuscript, but they also wanted this."

"What do you think it's for?" Derek asked.

"Zadkiel said it was like a third eye, a way to see. Maybe it's some kind of decoder." With that, Max held Zadkiel's stone up to the light, its emerald center gleaming, even brighter from the sunlight through the window.

"Wait! Max," Sam exclaimed. "Look… at the manuscript!"

Max glanced down at the table. There, on what had been a blank back page, a mysterious set of numbers appeared, illuminated in a fluorescent, blue-ish purple ink.

"What is that?!" Derek asked, leaning in closer. "Looks like our algebra homework, but even worse."

"It's some type of formula," Max said, shifting the stone around to reveal the complete set of figures on the page. "Maybe more like calculus; that's what my dad worked with, advanced mathematics."

"Do you think that's his handwriting?" Sam inquired. "It looks similar to the notes on the other pages."

"I think so," Max responded, flipping to the next page and the next. The blank back sides of each handwritten page were not blank at all, but filled with numbers, symbols, equations, and formulations.

"Dad must have done his initial calculations here, based on the findings of the monks. If he was looking to find where dark energy was leaking through, he must have known about their story, he must have thought there was something more to it."

"But how does that help us?" Derek asked. "We can't decipher all this—it's not like we're math wizards like your dad."

"Even if we could," Sam said, "your dad was a researcher, right? You said he worked in a lab; he had access to all sorts of equipment."

"Yeah, that's just it, even if we could make sense of this, whatever he created out of it, whatever experiment he attempted, was destroyed the night he went missing."

Derek rolled his eyes. "Bummer, and it's not like our school's science lab would be much help. Too bad there's not some kind of hack we could use," Derek muttered.

The crew sat quiet again. The manuscript lay open on the table, and alongside it, Max had laid the copy of Mr. Gabe's book on the strange medieval creatures, and a wad of tissues from his backpack. The late afternoon light shone brighter for a moment through the large windowpanes. Max turned toward it, as if the light itself was calling to him.

ASSSCCCHHHEEWWW!!

"Bless you," Sam said instinctively.

"Forget about it, Sam, this happens every time he looks—"

"WAIT!! Derek, you're a genius!!"

"Who, me? What did I say?"

"You said to look for a hack… *a shortcut.*"

"Yeah, I'm not following you, Max," Sam said, "what kind of hack could possibly take the place of all that research, all that expensive lab equipment?"

"That's just it, it doesn't require any equipment, it just requires a certain genetic tendency… PSR… photo sneeze reflex. You said it, Derek, it happens every time, like clockwork."

"Your ACHOO sneezing thing?" Derek asked, puzzled.

"Look, look here, both of you," Max said excitedly, shuffling through the illustrated pages in Mr. Gabe's book. "See! See here! These things, these time sucker things, supposedly come in when you are unaware, when you're drifting off to sleep or when you're starting to—"

"Sneeze!" said Sam."

"Yes! Yes!" Max exclaimed, as Sam began to slowly nod.

"I still don't get it," Derek said, completely confused.

"Listen," Max continued, "if daydreaming or sneezing is the precise moment *we* are most vulnerable, then that's the precise moment *they* are vulnerable, too. It's the moment they have to materialize, if just for a split second."

"Okay, I'm with you, and then what?" Sam asked, leaning in, eyes widening with interest.

"I don't exactly know. Like you said, Derek, it's a hack. It's a place to start. Proof that this place, and these creatures, exist."

"But these creatures, they appear, but they don't really take physical form, at least not for long," Sam questioned. "You can't *actually* hold on to them, right? Someone would have discovered that years ago."

"Yeah, Max, it would be like trying to grab the boogeyman in a nightmare."

"Correct," Max stated. "Normally they are in and out in a split second. Plus, these time thieves use that déjà vu trick to wipe your memory, make you forget so you wouldn't even notice. You'd have to be ready, waiting for it to happen."

"And then?" Sam continued.

"Well, if you know about them, and you're ready, you could *force* them to steal more life energy than they meant to," Max continued, still formulating his hypothesis.

"*Force them?* Why would you want them to steal your life energy? That makes no sense," Derek objected.

"It makes perfect sense! What if I were to sneeze enough times in a row that they consumed too much life force all at once? Instead of materializing for a nano second, maybe they would actually solidify and appear long enough to take a picture or gather some kind of evidence."

"Even if that's true, how would you force them to steal more energy?" Sam asked, still puzzled at the details of the plan.

"By sneezing! Over and over. These things are looking for 'food' so to speak, life force, right? Think of it like a mosquito, or better yet, a tick—once they latch on, you just keep pumping them with more and more, they won't be able to stop."

"That's a very interesting theory, Max," Sam said, mulling it over in her mind.

"More like disturbing," said Derek. "I vote we just wait for the old guy to wake back up."

"So how do you propose we test out this idea of yours?" Sam said with growing interest.

"Not how, where. At your place, Sam," Max replied. "It's ideal."

"My place, it's a loft apartment, how is that going to help?"

"What's out back?" Max asked, eyebrows raised.

"Just our back porch…"

"Just a back porch?" Max asked. "Or perhaps a gateway… your solarium!"

CHAPTER 11

"**A**re we all set?" Max asked.

"Sure, I guess, as set as we can be," Sam replied a bit nervously, holding her cell phone up in anticipation. "Let's hope this works."

Afternoon light was already streaming through the brightly lit curved glass of Sam's sun porch, her favorite reading spot in the second story apartment she shared with her father and one cat. Sam's dad added the solarium after the divorce and she used it as a getaway, cuddling up on the soft rattan couch after school to soak up warmth and information.

"What do you want me to do?" Derek asked. "Shouldn't I have a baseball bat or something? I can whack-a-mole this thing if it shows up."

"NO!" Max replied. "We're simply after evidence, we just need to prove the theory, something we can take to the authorities, or back to Professor Gutt if he recovers. You can just hand me Kleenex."

Max could already feel the tingle building in his nose, that familiar twitch that comes just before a sneeze.

"Sam, here, move those plants over here, that will help even more," Max instructed, motioning to the daisies and marigolds that sat in planters near the windows.

"Just don't look directly at the sun," Sam warned.

"I'm not," Max reassured her. "I'm looking just to the left of—"

"*ACHOO!!*"

It was a whopper of a sneeze, but nothing happened. Max looked skyward again.

"*ACHOO!! ACHOO!!*" Max repeated, his nose already starting to redden.

"So where's the Boggart dude?" Derek asked.

"Give it a hot minute," Max said with some annoyance. Keeping his face skyward, soon one sneeze followed another.

Sam gently shook one of the flowerpots near Max. "See if this helps."

"ACHOO!!"

"Yes, keep it going," Max instructed, turning to look toward the light again.

"ACHOO!! ACHOO!! ACHOO!!"

Eyes watering, Max took a quick breath. "Just hand me some more Kleenex," Max said, motioning to Derek. "I've got more in my backpack."

"Here, take this," Sam offered, placing Mr. Jitters, her long haired Siamese cat squarely in Max's lap. "See if this makes a difference."

"Are you trying to kill me?" Max said, eyes and nose now dripping like a leaky outdoor faucet.

"ACHOO!! ACHOO!! ACHOO!! ACHOO!! ACHOO!!"

"I don't know, Max," said Derek after about ten minutes. "You must have sneezed fifty times."

Derek kept counting out loud. Fifty-nine… sixty… seventy… eighty… Max felt his ribs starting to ache. Ninety-nine… one hundred…

"Max, I'm not sure…" Sam began to say, a look of concern coming over her face.

"Hand me my inhaler," Max commanded Derek, "it's in the rear zippered pouch."

"Max, stop, you're starting to wheeze," Sam pleaded. "This isn't worth it."

Max's head was now reeling. No longer able to stand, he plopped down on the couch.

"ACHOO!! ACHOO!! ACHOO!!"

Just then, Max felt something, a wisp, a movement, a flash out of the corner of his eye.

"Wait!" Max said between gasps. "Sam, Derek, I know how they did it!" Max shouted, gasping deeply to avoid blacking out.

"How *who* did *what?*"

"The monks. The Benedictine monks! There were one hundred and twenty-six of them, right?"

Though Derek struggled with algebra, he had a keen memory for statistics, thanks to his obsession with baseball cards. "Yeah, that sounds right," he said, recalling their previous discussions. "Why?"

"Because that's how they got in! *They all sneezed at once!* One hundred and twenty-six sneezes!" The sudden burst of insight re-energized Max.

"ACHOO!! ACHOO!! ACHOO!!"

"Well, you're almost there, one hundred twenty-two, one hundred twenty-three..." Derek said.

"Sam, get your phone ready!" Max shouted.

A small wind seemed to kick up out of nowhere, stirring the leaves on the plants around them.

"Max, you're looking really queasy," Sam warned.

"ACHOO!!"

"One hundred and twenty-four," Derek called out. Something seemed to flash by, like a fast-moving cloud blocking the sun.

"ACHOO!!"

"One hundred and twenty-five." A high-pitched squealing noise suddenly rang out, like that of a small, frightened pig.

"ACHOO!!"

"One hundred and twenty-six..." Derek declared with finality.

Then it happened.

A distorted, squished-up face appeared out of thin air, directly in front of Derek. Green, spindly arms jutting out in every direction.

"Uh, Max..."

"Achoo!"

"Max, I think that's enough," Derek said in disbelief, pointing at the whirling tangle of arms and legs in front of him. "Look!"

Max blinked for a second, clearing his eyes.

"Ahhhh!!" The hideous face of the creature took full form for all of a second, but a second was all Max needed.

"Gotcha!" Max grabbed a thin, bony arm as the creature shrieked, twisting and turning madly. The piercing scream startled Max so much that he nearly let go of the howling beast.

"It's one of them, it's a Boggart!" Max exclaimed. "Sam, quick—take a picture!" Max doubled down on his hold, his body flailing wildly from side to side, all the while desperately trying to maintain his grip. Sam held up her phone only to have it knocked out of her hand by a spinning arm.

"Derek, don't... just... stand there! Help me!"

"Then let go, idiot!" Derek pleaded helplessly.

But Max wouldn't. Not after this much work, and not after knowing full well what these thieves were up to. The whirling bandit clutched and clawed, trying desperately to retreat down what appeared to be an oversized wormhole that had opened around it. Max worked to regain his grip as he felt a powerful suction, like an enormous vacuum hose, pulling him closer to the mysterious hole.

"I'm losing him," Max shouted, as he lunged for a belt around the waist of the creature. The sound of the gaping vacuum howled like a tornado as the Boggart retreated back into it. Max felt himself slipping, spiraling downward into the black opening, unwilling to let go.

"Nooooo!" Derek screamed, flinging himself at Max. His left hand latched hard onto Max's backpack, finding a hold on one the loose straps, his other arm grabbing tightly around Max's waist.

"Oh no you don't! Not without me!" Sam exclaimed, wrapping her arms around Derek's knees, shutting her eyes tightly as she braced for what was about to happen.

And then they were gone.

CHAPTER 12

A speeding blur of muted blues and grays streaked by them as they all tumbled downward, head over heels in what seemed an endless freefall. All the while the Boggart pawed wildly at Max, who had managed to grab another of the Boggart's six arms. Derek held on as well, praying that, against all odds this was some illusion—perhaps the result of a fever or a food-borne illness. Maybe the shepherd's pie, he told himself, recalling the Tuesday menu in the school cafeteria. Sam winced, trying not to think at all, the constant whirling making her motion-sick. The twisting, turning bundle of arms and legs spun wildly out of control as they all clutched onto each other—and to any hope for survival.

Thud!

The sudden landing knocked the wind out of Max. He gasped hard to draw in a breath as Derek let out a slight groan. All was quiet. The spiraling mosaic of muted colors had come to a complete halt. Max felt dizzy from the loss of air and inhaled rapidly to make up for it. This hyperventilation only worsened the problem, so he lay back flat on the ground, trying to breathe deeply. The air smelled musty, and what little light there was glowed dimly from deep within the walls of what appeared to be some sort of underground grotto—a small subterranean chamber about twenty to thirty feet wide. Derek groaned again.

"Derek? You okay?"

"Derek?"

There was no answer.

"Derek! C'mon, are you alright?"

Another long pause, then Derek slowly spoke. "I think I broke my butt. Is that possible? Are there such things as butt bones?" He hoisted himself up from the chamber floor, dusting himself off.

"Whew!" Max breathed a sigh of relief. "And what about Sam? She stayed back, right?"

"Nope!" came the familiar voice. "Unfortunately, we all took the same taxi ride," she said, rubbing her own backside. "And yes, Derek, you can definitely break your butt."

"Sam!" Max exclaimed, exasperated. "Why in the world would you—"

"Hey! I'm not going to just sit back and watch you two disappear through some portal. And besides, if you're going to find this Nemesis place, you're going to need a good detective."

"Alright, fair enough," replied Max, his head still reeling.

"You can start by detecting where we're at," Derek said, lighting the cavern up as best he could with the tiny light from his cell phone. "Looks like some sort of dungeon."

In the hazy light of the cavernous tunnel, Derek thought he saw something strange moving ever so slowly, steadily rising and falling, underneath Max.

"M-M-Max," he stammered, backing away while pointing at Max's feet. "What's *that*?" Max, having sat up, on what felt like a warm, soft pillow, now glanced between his spread legs.

"Yow!!"

He jumped up as fast as he could. Below him lay the massive Boggart that had fortunately landed ahead of Max, cushioning his fall and sending the other two bouncing off to the left and right. What was left of the creature looked more like a slightly squashed green marshmallow sandwich.

Gross as it all was, Max breathed a sigh of relief. At least now there wouldn't be a thrashing Boggart to ward off, and they could focus their attention on just where in the world, or out of the world, they might be. Max sniffed the air. It smelled familiar, like his grandmother's basement with all the musty back issues of *National Geographic*—a smell he likened to puppy breath, but slightly worse, like day-old gym socks. In the distance, he could hear the hum of what sounded like farm machinery. Max looked up at the wormhole they had just fallen through. A sign above it read:

Magnetic Wave Tunnel #64787.

Hmmmm, Max marveled. *Magnetic waves… like energy lines, invisible ones.* Max wondered if that meant those creatures used them somehow, like highways of sorts. He had a vague recollection of some theory about all this from watching the Discovery Channel and reading *Popular Science,* two pastimes he generally kept to himself. Max looked down at the now unconscious Boggart, lying sprawled on its back with a half dazed look on its three-eyed face. Max had never seen nor even imagined such a weird-looking creature. Its six arms were each a different length, protruding from its body at odd angles in every direction, like the trunk of an old, dead pine tree. It had an equal number of legs, two main ones on which it apparently walked, and two sets of other ones, which kept the top-heavy troll from tipping completely over. Its skin had the appearance of a reptile, a snake perhaps—or was it more like the hide of a rhino? In two of its hands lay a flashing device, something that looked like a glass bazooka, filled with tubes of what looked like neon lights. At its tip was a long, narrow cone, needle shaped, that looked like it was made of stainless steel.

"This must be what the Boggarts use to steal time, *the Extractors,*" Max declared.

Derek and Sam had now cautiously pulled up alongside Max, peering intently at the creature as well.

"Look," said Sam, "there's some sort of readout on the side of it, like a display panel or something." Max picked up the Extractor and felt its weight, flipping it over a couple of times to have a closer look.

"There," Sam repeated. "Look what it says… 126."

With a shock, Max realized it was the exact number of breaths the oversized leech had sucked from his lungs while sneezing and blown into the device.

"Well, this is great, Max, just terrific. *Now* what do we do?" Derek moaned in total disgust, the wet cave-like floor soaking through the bottom of his thick denim jeans. "Thanks to your 'theory,' we're stuck in some kind of underworld sewer with six-armed, six-legged mutants and—"

"Shhh!" Max held a finger to his lips and cocked his head sideways to listen. Derek opened his mouth to speak but Max again hushed him with a gesture.

"Listen!" Max put his ear against the cavern wall. "Do you hear it? That humming sound?"

As he spoke, a low eerie sound seemed to come from one of the tunnel openings ahead of them, a distant rumble, like faraway thunder or the beginning stirrings of a volcano.

"Yeah! I do," Sam said intently. "What do you think it is?"

Derek stood by sulking, uninterested, his gaze fixed solely on the spiraling opening they had just fallen though, now high up above them in the chamber ceiling. Its soft, cloud-like edges swirled around a deep sea of dark blue.

"Hey, guys…" he said pointing upward in an effort to get their attention.

"If this place is what it looks like," Max continued, "it could be the tunnel systems the Boggarts use to come and go, to deliver their stolen goods… the ones that go into—"

"The Time Vault!" Sam finished his sentence.

"Yeah," Max nodded, excited that Sam was following his train of thought. "The one Professor Gutt was describing. Maybe that's what's making that low grinding sound; they're slowly opening a massive vault door and—"

"Or maybe it's the sound of innocent children being sacrificed to some dungeon volcano god," Derek interrupted. "Tell me you two are kidding! Let's just climb back out the way we came in. I've got a really bad feeling about this, Max."

Just then, the spiraling dark hole above them disappeared.

"Oh! Great!" Derek moaned.

"Forget about it, Derek, that's not even the direction we're heading," Max insisted.

"The direction we're heading? The direction we should be heading is to an elevator shaft straight back home. And speaking of heading, how is heading down one of these tunnels any better? For all we know, this 'tunnel' could be the throat of a huge underground snake. Max, we have *no idea* what's down there! Maybe we should do the opposite, try to climb our way back out. Just get out and get help!"

"Help? What kind of help would you suggest?" Max shot back. "Tell our parents? Call the FBI? Which government agency is in charge of fighting phantom thieves from some invisible dark side?"

"Max is right, Derek," Sam insisted, pleading with him. "Think about it, even if we could get back right now somehow, how crazy would we all sound? Remember the professor? He spent his life fighting this thing and no one helped him one bit. That's how he ended up in my Lifespan ward, alone and abandoned, because no one believed him. Besides, aren't you at all curious? This stuff is *really* happening… first the changelings, now the Boggarts, and now this place… it's really true."

"And if this much is true, then maybe all of it is true," Max stated with an air of urgency. "Maybe, somehow, my dad is down here, too. The professor said so. I can't leave—I *won't* leave—until I find out."

Derek paused for a moment, as if to absorb everything Max and Sam had said. The cavern air felt cool and damp in the dim light, the musty smell of uncertainty seeping from every crevice in the walls. Max could see that his words had sunk in, but that fact alone didn't make Derek feel any better.

"Okay," Derek finally said, "I'm on board with that. Let's see what we can find out about your dad, and maybe even that vault thing, and then let's get the heck out of here. The sooner the better."

"Agreed, so are we good?" Max said.

"Yep, all in," Sam said with a thumbs-up, Derek nodded along in agreement.

"Great!" Max said. "Now all we need to do is find our way out of here. Chances are one of these passages will take us closer to the source of that sound."

"There's got to be at least a dozen ways out of here," Derek said, refocusing his attention to the task at hand. "Who's to say which tunnel is the right one? Wait, I got an idea!" He wet his forefinger with the tip of his tongue, holding it high in the air, as if to detect the direction of the wind.

"What are you doing?" Sam asked, puzzled.

"I saw this in a movie once about caves, it always leads to the outside."

"I'm not so sure that applies here," Sam insisted.

"Hmmm," Max said, walking back and forth in front of several of the tunnel openings. "I can hear that humming sound coming from at least half of those openings." As he walked, he gently tapped the front glass portion of the Extractor device in the palm of his hand.

"Hey, what about the Extractor itself, Max?" Sam suggested. "Is there something on there that could help? It has all those buttons and readings."

"Let's see," Max said, flipping it over and turning it from end to end. Alternating blips of red, green, orange, and yellow flashed and pulsated as Max pointed the device in various directions.

"Huh," Max said quietly. "I think you may be on to something, Sam. There must be a way the Time Extractor links to the Time Vault. Maybe one of these lights serves as a type of homing beacon in case the Boggart gets lost along the way."

"Like a GPS system?" she ventured.

"Exactly! See, notice how this yellow one gets brighter when I move forward this way? And then it dims when I step back." Max demonstrated the move, crisscrossing the chamber floor, stepping over the flattened-out Boggart several times in the process, all the while carefully monitoring the yellow light.

"Now watch, it gets brighter when I go near this opening." Max moved toward a triangular-shaped crevice in the wall, not much higher than himself and very narrow at the entrance. "If we head this way, the sound not only gets louder, but the light shines brighter as we go. That should also help us to see better."

Max seemed pleased with the accomplishment. "Alright, let's think about this like a video game. We're just going to take our time, figure out each level, until we get our answers. Then it's game over."

Derek shuddered at Max's choice of words. "It'll be over, all right," he mumbled under his breath. "I'm just hoping there's a replay button in case we lose."

CHAPTER 13

Max took the lead, motioning the others to follow along. Hurrying to catch up, Derek stepped over the pancaked Boggart still lying in the middle of the cavern. As he did, his rear foot caught hold of a woven belt wrapped tightly around its waist. Derek fell with a *thunk* as he landed face-first on the wet, muddy floor. A thick sludge of goo oozed through the space between his two front teeth.

"Gross!" he yelled, wiping the mud off his face, and then rubbing his hands across the front of his jeans. He flung the excess sludge against the cave walls with a flick of his hands.

"Are you alright?" Sam asked, "What did you trip on?"

"Not sure," Derek replied, leaning down for a closer look. He unbuckled the coarsely woven belt, tugging hard until, at last, it came loose from underneath the thick torso of the limp-bodied Boggart. He examined the sturdy, boar hair-like fabric, about three inches wide, lined with different-sized pockets. Each pocket contained a shiny, metallic-looking tool, in all various shapes and sizes—like the kind a carpenter or electrician might wear.

"Maybe some of this techno-gizmo stuff will come in handy," Derek said with a hint of hope in his voice.

"C'mon, Derek," Max urged. "There's no telling how much time we have. The light keeps glowing brighter this way…" Max's voice trailed off as he entered the triangle-shaped opening and disappeared. Sam followed closely on his heels. Derek quickly fell behind as he inspected the many objects on the belt, strapping it, like a newfound trophy, around his thin, athletic frame.

"Derek! C'mon, keep up," Max insisted as he moved forward along the tunnel, ducking to avoid taking any more hard knocks to the head.

He listened for Derek's footsteps and squinted, looking back, using only the glow of the Time Extractor to get a better look.

"Sam, is Derek behind you?"

"I think so," she replied. "He was messing with a belt he found."

"Hey! Slow down, I can't see!" said Derek, as he felt his way along the moist, rough walls, the glow from Max's Time Extractor provided the only light available to see.

"Max? You there?"

"Derek! Over here!"

Derek pulled up alongside Max and Sam. "Check this out!" he pointed to his belt, wrapped twice around his waist.

"Nice!" Max said, acknowledging Derek's find. "Now let's stay tight moving forward; we can't afford to lose anybody. These walls seem to be made of something that gives off a little glow, but it's not enough to see very well."

With that, Max scanned the wet walls of the tunnel up and down, pointing the tip of the Extractor at various rocks and outcroppings, each one reflecting different amounts of light, causing ghost-like shadows to rise and fall.

"Wait! What's that?" Sam pointed out, motioning to a carved-out opening just ahead. The front of it was lined with metal bars, rising from floor to ceiling, about six inches apart.

"Weird!" Max stated, as he moved the Extractor toward the opening.

"What is it?" Sam asked.

"The Extractor. The light gets really bright when I point it closer to those bars. I don't get it… it doesn't make sense."

"Of course, it doesn't make sense!"

Max spun around at the sound of the strange voice.

"It makes no sense, because you're an Earthling, a 'fleshy,' a carbon copy, so to speak, running at a steady 98.6 degrees with eight possible blood types, opposable thumbs, and an average life span of seventy-four years—if you're male, that is. What else do you want to know?"

"Who said that!" Max demanded, grasping the Time Extractor tighter and moving even closer toward the caged opening.

"Hey! Put that thing down, you're shining it right in my eyes and you don't have the safety on. You could vaporize someone if you're not careful."

"Yeah? Well just who the heck are you?" Derek shouted back, equally surprised at the sight.

"Humphries' the name. Now what's your game? Aren't you a little far from home?"

Max motioned to Derek and Sam to stay back as he inched forward. Probing the dark with the Time Extractor light, he exposed the face of yet another unsightly Boggart. Only this one was sat locked inside of what looked like a crude prison cell, carved out of the side of the tunnel wall.

"Congratulations! You spotted me. Not only that, but you managed to make it to this side. That's farther than most." The Boggart leaned closer toward the prison bars and peered intently at Max.

"Say! I bet you're the one they're all talking about, aren't you? The boy with the book! Rumor had it that you got a bit banged up by a few changelings. Yet here you are—you and your half-pint friends there."

"Hey!" said Derek in outrage.

"Yeah!" shouted Sam.

Ignoring their outburst, the Boggart shook his head. "All this talk about the big threat to the Vault, and look at you three. You're about as dangerous as a night light."

Max stepped back, the Extractor still pointing squarely ahead. Shouldering it up to his right side, he used his free left hand to feel for the wet wall behind him. He leaned back against it, then propping himself up, held his eye down the barrel, as if to intimidate the caged inmate.

"Just tell me where we are!" Max demanded.

"And to hear all you Fleshies go on and on about manners. How about returning the courtesy and introducing yourselves?"

The request caught Max completely off-guard.

"Introducing?" he said, dropping the Extractor back down to waist level.

"Yes," replied the Boggart, "introducing yourself, like in your world when people say,"—and here, he lowered his voice, tilting his fat chin down and acting as if he were being very formal, "'hello, my name is…'"

"Okay, fair enough." Max let the Extractor drop down along his side with the strap around his neck. "You said it was Humphries? Right?"

"Correct-o, sir," he replied to Max.

"Well, I'm Max... Maxwell Kellerman. And this is Derek. And this is Sam. We're from Providence."

"Rhode Island?" he shrieked with delight. "I know it well! The Ocean State. Little Rhody. From the Dutch 'Rood Eylandt,' meaning 'red island.' The state motto is 'hope,' a bit ironic if you ask me, since you could certainly use some right now..."

"Yeah, yeah," Derek said impatiently. "Okay, we told you who we are, now tell us *where* we are!"

"Why should I tell you anything? You're just another bunch of foolhardy wannabes that come bounding down here every few hundred years thinking you're going to empty the vault, save your world and gain instant stardom. Well, I've got news for you: It doesn't work that way. You're going to fail just like they all did."

"Who's they?" asked Max, probing further. "Are you talking about the monks?"

"Oh, so we've already graduated from boy wonder to boy genius, have we? Well, the monks were the exception. And they didn't stop it, they just managed to disrupt it for a few hundred years. And they paid rather dearly if I recall correctly. But alas, the transformation is back on schedule. There's no stopping it this time."

Both Derek and Sam eyed each other nervously, then glanced back over to Max, who now held the Extractor back up to his waist.

"Oh, and while we're at it, one more tidbit of bad news: Abaddon knows you're here."

"Abaddon!" Max's thoughts flashed back to Zadkiels' warning.

"Rings a bell, does it? Well, it should! And trust me when I say he has plans for you. If he wasn't so busy getting prepared for entry, he'd probably be here right now turning your soul into vapor."

Derek swallowed hard. "So this dude's for real? I mean, I thought this stuff was all made up."

"Made up like what? Fear? Hate? Revenge? Made up stuff like that? Well, he's the one who whispers in your sleep and plants seeds of doubt in your mind. And once there, they grow until all is destroyed. It's slow and gradual, but very effective. And in the end, Abaddon gets what Abaddon wants."

"And what's that?" Max asked.

"Power. Control. Dominion. Over everything, pure and simple. His rules are everyone's rules. And humans are what can tip the balance in his favor; your world is the doorway to realms he can't reach right now."

"So… if you're so big on this guy, what're you doing here?" Sam asked, emboldened by the fact that the Boggart was securely behind bars.

"Sharp one, that one there," said Humphries, pointing a long, bony finger at Sam.

"Hey, just answer the question," Max said. "Why aren't you helping this Abaddon guy blast into our planet and wreck the world?"

The air grew silent.

"I got fired," he mumbled.

"You got what?" Derek laughed out loud. "Excuse me?" he asked, cupping his ear as he leaned closer. "Couldn't quite hear that. You got what?"

"Fired!" Humphries admitted with an air of exasperation, all six of his different length arms waving wildly in the air, as if for emphasis.

"So, tell me," Derek went on, now cockier than ever, "how does a time-sucking, low-life like you get fired?"

"Even here we have rules. And Boggarts are strictly forbidden from stealing time—for their own consumption, that is. That's why I only took enough to help me do my job better."

"Oh, this is really getting good!" Derek shook his head in disbelief. "Not just a time-sucking thief but a time-sucking Boy Scout just trying to help his fellow slime. Max, are you getting all this?"

Max nodded somberly. "Yeah. So let me ask you this," he said to Humphries. "If we let you out of here, will you help us?"

"Are you crazy?" Derek shouted. "Like we don't already have enough trouble?"

"Help you what?" asked Humphries. "Empty the Time Vault?"

"No. Destroy the Time Vault."

"You *are* joking, right? Destroy the Time Vault? Do you have a death wish or something? Have you heard of Michael the Archangel? Or how about Gabriel? They went into early retirement without beating this thing."

Sam eyed Max cautiously, a look of growing concern in her expression. Max gave her a quick, knowing nod, as if to say *don't worry, I got this.*

"Okay, you're right, so let's just say we just skip the whole idea," Max said with a shrug. "Then what happens to you? Do you just get left behind when they leave for Earth?"

"Oh, I see where you're going with this. But the answer is still no! I'll take eternity here over what's going to happen to you. You have a high price on your head and I, for one, would rather stay put than be vaporized in the Abyss."

"Just exactly how long are you here for?" Derek piped in.

"Uh… well… counting the time I've already served? That leaves 12,656 Earth years, give or take a few."

"Well, it's your choice," Max said matter-of-factly, throwing up his hands. "We're moving on with or without you. Maybe the next group of foolhardy wannabes will find you here in a few thousand years."

With that, Max gathered up his backpack, slung the Time Extractor over his shoulder and prepared to head out.

"Wait! Wait just a minute!" Humphries insisted, reaching out three of his right hands in protest. "Perhaps you may have a point, shrewd Earthies that you are. Heh, heh, heh," he continued with a nervous laugh. "How about you let me out, and I'll take you to the Gates of Ishtar and not one step farther—from there you can see The Vault. There are way too many Narks beyond there."

"To where we can actually see The Vault? How can I know you'll keep your word?"

Dropping two of his bottom right arms, Humphries extended his top right hand, glistening with a thin, oily looking sweat. "Let's shake on it. A Boggart never breaks a handshake, especially when it's the top right hand."

Max turned back to Derek and Sam, who had been staring the entire time back and forth between all three of the Boggart's eyes, trying to detect any hint of deception.

"Hard to say," said Sam, as Humphries managed a cheesy looking grin, "but I say give him a chance."

"Yeah," Derek agreed, "cause just remember, you can always use the Time Extractor to suck the living daylights out of him if he makes one wrong move."

Humphries swallowed hard, a process which made him shift colors from green to light orange, and back again. "Now, just as a reminder, be careful with that thing… the fact that you're following the glowing yellow light, which leads to other Boggarts, only proves you have no idea what you're doing. May I suggest you simply use the key?"

"What key is that?" Max asked.

"The one on his belt," Humphries answered, pointing to one of the devices arrayed around Derek's waist. "Here, I'll show you, but we gotta make this quick. We're overdue for a patrol and that would not be good."

Max nodded to Derek to remove the shiny, tube-shaped cylinder and give it to Humphries. The imprisoned Boggart took it through the bars and, with his two longest arms, waved the tiny cylinder in front of a square stone pad attached to the wall next to the jail cell. The pad lit up into a glowing grid composed of nine distinct colors, each blinking and changing rapidly, along with the nine glowing stripes that appeared on the jail key. Finally, the colors on the pad and the key matched, making a *ching* sound.

Then the prison bars began vibrating and slowly turning in place. With each rotation, the vibrations increased with speed, until suddenly they dissolved into thin air.

"Thank you, dear gentlemen and gentlelady," the Boggart said with a bow, grinning broadly as he stepped out into his newfound freedom. Noticing their astonished looks, he commented apologetically, "Sorry, my English has not been updated for a while. What I meant to say was—"

"No," Derek interrupted. "What just happened to those…" pointing to where the bars once were.

"Oh, those! They operate on a secret frequency. Technically speaking, they were never there at all, a form of contracted negative density, but that's another story."

"AAAAHHHHH!!! LET US OUT!!!"

Max spun around at the sound.

The sudden disappearance of the jail cell bars sparked an outcry. Ahead in the tunnel, arms and legs jutted out in every direction, revealing additional cages upon cages of imprisoned Boggarts, each wailing loudly to Humphries to set them free as well. Humphries turned toward Max and rolled his one big eyebrow.

"What about them?" Max asked, pointing toward the other inmates. "What are they all doing here?"

"Let 'em rot!" Humphries muttered. "They're a bunch of common thieves."

"But you are, too!" Derek said in utter disbelief.

"Oh, I may look like them, and I've stolen my share of time," Humphries said, pointing toward one of the tunnel exits, "but *I* can be trusted."

CHAPTER 14

"**S**o you've actually *seen* this Time Vault?" Max asked as Humphries led them out of the tunnel and onto a wide ledge that lined the very top of a humongous central cavern. The sprawling expanse stretched out for at least a mile, like a huge church cathedral with rocky spires resembling organ pipes that jutted up along the edges in the distance. Derek walked wide-eyed along behind them, not watching where he was going.

"Watch it, Derek," Sam cautioned, grabbing his belt and giving him a sharp pull backward. Small rocks and pebbles cascaded down, bouncing into the darkness below.

"Wow, that was close. Thanks, Sam," Derek said, a quick shudder passing through him, before turning his attention back on the path.

"Seen it?" Humphries stated, unaware of the near fall behind him. "I was once the Master Time Keeper in charge of over three divisions of Boggarts. But that was several hundred years ago. The Vault has undergone a lot of modifications since then. It's hard to keep up with it all. Some of it is automated now—these younger Boggarts, a lot of attitude, no respect for all the work that went on before them."

"But you still know the way there, right?" Derek's eyes practically begged Humphries to give them a simple and direct answer, one free from dire warnings.

"Yes, of course. They would never change the actual location, that would be ridiculous! It would mean disrupting everything. Time is a delicate thing. The whole stealing and storing process gets very involved, much like winemaking, only with much more skill and craftsmanship—" Humphries stopped abruptly, raising his head to sniff the air.

"Get down—now!"

Max, Derek, and Sam fell instantly onto the wet, cold stone path. The entire surface had a thin, slippery film on it, like the inside of an aquarium that has not been cleaned for several weeks. Max inched up close behind Humphries.

"What is it?" Max whispered.

"Narks. I can smell them, they're so disgusting. Why, if I ever get my hands around one of their bony necks…"

A blast of wind suddenly struck their backs, sending them flying like June bugs against the wall that lined the enormous cavern.

Whoosh! Whoosh!

A startling flapping noise thundered just above them. Max craned his neck to glimpse a winged, two-headed beast, diving at them, its nostrils flared and claws extended.

"Into the cracks!" Humphries shouted.

Max, Derek, and Sam half crawled, slipping and sliding along the wall, looking for any available crevice to wedge themselves securely out of reach.

SCCCRRRREEEEEEAAAAKKK!

One of the creature's long razor-sharp talons whisked by, searing the rock with its tip, leaving a permanent long scar etched into the solid stone wall. Finding a narrow opening, Max thrust himself inside. To his surprise, Derek was already tightly packed inside.

"Ouch! That's my foot!" Derek cried.

"Move on back, Derek, Humphries is still out there!"

"I can't! I'm already wedged in here! And so is Sam!"

"Sam!?"

"Yeah, I'm alright, just can't… quite… breathe."

"Hold on," Max instructed. "I've gotta get Humphries."

A high-pitched screech pierced the air as Max turned to see the creature, talons outstretched, circling back to make another dive, this time on Humphries.

AWWRRRKK!

The cry grew louder as Max wasted no time, grabbing Humphries and pulling him up on his feet with all his might. "C'mon, get in there!" Max pushed hard against Humphries' hard, walrus-like exterior, leaning his shoulders in and pushing with both feet.

"Okay, I'm almost in," Humphries said, sucking in his bloated belly as best he could.

AWWRRRKK!!

The screech echoed directly behind Max. "GET… IN… THERE…" he yelled, throwing all his small frame into Humphries' backside.

WOOOSSSHHH!

The air gushed again, the talons scraping across the face of the narrow opening, just glancing Max's backpack, leaving a small tear across the top.

"Whew!" Max breathed a sigh of relief. "That was close."

"Close?" came a muffled cry. "Things can't get much closer…" Max could tell from her voice that Sam was on the edge of panic. "Max, I can't budge," she said. "I think I'm stuck, and I still can't… draw in… much air…" Her voice faded off.

"Max, what are we going to do? I'm stuck, too. Even if we could move, we can't go back out there and we can't stay here?"

"Humphries, any ideas?" Max urged.

"There is another set of tunnels, the old system, at the other end of this crevice. If we can just work our way through here," he said, wiggling a bit. "I can squeeze myself thinner, but your two friends here are gumming up the works."

Max's thoughts raced. *We didn't come this far to get stuck in some stupid wall*, he thought. Scenes of their time together flashed before him, late night stories around a campfire, the final stretch of that walkathon, the time at the county fair where they watched Derek try to catch that greasy little baby pig…

Wait! That's it, Max thought.

"I hope you two like Humphries, you're about to get very acquainted with him," Max yelled over to the pair. "Sam, Derek, if you can, reach over and wipe your hands on any part of Humphries you can find."

"What?" Derek questioned.

"Just do it. You too, Sam, can you hear me?"

"Yeah, I think I can get one hand free," she replied weakly.

"That's it, now just wipe your hand all over his skin and then coat yourself with it, anywhere that's touching the wall where you're stuck. It should work like a lubricating fluid, like that greased pig Derek could never…" he continued.

"Okay... working... on... it..." she gasped in short gasps.

"Same here," Derek joined in.

"Wait! I think my other arm is loose!" Sam shouted excitedly. "I think I can move some too now."

"How about you, Derek?"

"Yeah, I think I'm good," he replied.

"Humphries, go ahead and give them both a push, see if you can get them through to the other side."

"If you insist," Humphries replied matter-of-factly. With that, he stiffened up his body, wedging himself even more tightly against the two sides of the crevice, and then, with all three of his powerful right hands, pushed hard against Derek, who in turn pushed against Sam.

"OWW! OWW!! WAIT!!"

SLOOOOSHH!

Suddenly the path ahead opened up as both Derek and Sam passed like kidney stones through the narrow crack, out the other side, then down a wet, slippery rock face onto a spongy, moss-covered floor. Humphries sucked in his gut, stretching himself taller and thinner, and grabbing Max's hand, pulled himself through as well. Sliding down, the final two tumbled, then plopped, onto the spongy surface, right next to Derek and Sam.

Max, Derek, and Sam sat, dazed for a moment, Sam still collecting her breath.

"Wow!" she finally muttered. "I don't think I'll try that again." She gave a grateful nod towards Max.

"Yeah, agreed," Max said. "We're only going to get so many near misses."

"Derek, you okay?"

"Hey, look at this!" Derek's attention had already moved on. He was now up on his feet, moving along the smaller interior cave walls. "You say this was some old Boggart highway system?" Derek asked. "'Cause it looks like the subway tunnels on the T," he said, referring to the subway system they had ridden together on numerous class trips to Boston. The walls stood covered from floor to ceiling with weird writings and symbols. One of them showed what looked like a smaller Boggart with the middle finger of its middle hand pointing up.

"Boggies!" Humphries said, shaking his head in exasperation at the scribbled markings. "Young, restless Boggarts with nothing better to do than deface public property. It's a shame."

"Uh, where are we again?" Max asked hesitantly.

Humphries stood up, brushed himself off, and in a voice more befitting a history teacher, offered the threesome the following explanation:

"Before the big renovation in the main chamber, these caves and interconnecting tunnels were the main means of travel. Now everyone uses the wide, open ledges we were just on. They were carved into the chamber walls to make it easier and quicker to descend down to the Vault. Think of it as one of your modern superhighways. It saves a lot of time traveling to the Vault, but it also leaves us exposed to Narks, as you just experienced.

"Narks?" Sam repeated, now almost fully recovered. "I guess those would have to be those—"

"Dirty, disgusting, oversized dragonflies—that's right. They patrol the central chamber looking for suspicious activity, such as you three… whomever they can sink their claws into. What are you using now? Oh, that's right… drones! Same difference. They spy on you, rat you out and even haul you off to the Chamber Tribunal for a rather hasty trial—one which always ends with a guilty verdict."

"But what's with all these rules and flying police dragons?" Derek demanded. "Why do they care about justice in a place like this?"

"Oh, don't get me wrong. They don't care at all about justice. It's all about enforcement… crowd control so to speak! That's why the verdict is always guilty. It keeps everyone in fear. That way there's no chance of someone messing things up and ruining the plan."

"That would be the plan to get out of here, right? To get to our world?" Max asked.

"Right. 'The Great Transformation' as they call it," Humphries said in a high pitched, exaggerated voice, gesturing as if he were selling tickets to a carnival show.

Max shook his head in bewilderment. "I don't get it. Why would they even want to go to Earth? Won't they be the same miserable beasts once they materialize?"

"Wow, where even to start," Humphries replied, rolling all three of his eyes up to the top of his thick unibrow. "They don't even know what they want, they're just promised things, bloodletting, human possession, torture, pillaging—for them it's like a trip to the amusement park."

"Promised? By whom?"

"Who else? Abaddon. Like I said, your world is but a steppingstone to what he really wants."

"Which is?"

"Revenge, payback, evening up an old score. He may be the ruler of Nemesis, but the real estate he really wants is Empyrean."

Empyrean? Max thought, remembering his visit with Zadkiel.

"Wait! I thought things down here on the lower level can't cross the line to the upper levels?" Max protested.

"Wow! Who told you that?" Humphries said, obviously impressed. "As a rule, that's true, but just don't tell that to Abbadon. After all, he was once from there."

Max leaned his back against the moist, mossy wall, pulled his knees up to his chest, resting his chin there while he gathered his thoughts. He wondered how he had managed to get himself, and his two best friends, into this jam. Had he just been reckless, or was he somehow losing his mind, still locked in some dream? After all, the whole idea of talking to a six-handed, three-eyed, time-stealing creature in some dark dimension seemed beyond absurd. Yet here he was. Derek, who never seemed to ponder much except the exact time and location of his next meal, was busy tracing the words etched on the cave wall with his finger.

"Is this *really* Boggart graffiti?" he asked.

Humphries nodded, "Yep, swear on my mother's egg pile. But they're just kids, only in their two-hundreds."

"Wow!" Derek exclaimed, amazed at all the artwork. "Sam, you should try your hand at this, you're good at—"

"Forget about it, Derek," Sam said, getting up slowly and wiping the remnants of Humphries' slime coat off her hands, knees, and shoulders with a piece of loose moss she took off the cave floor. "We need to get out of here."

"Yeah, where to next, Humphries?" Max asked. "You said you're familiar with these passages."

"Every one of these small rooms are like connecting hubs, each with two or more exits. Some lead to the dump, others lead to the incinerator, some to the main chamber floor and some to the Abyss." He shuddered, turning slightly orange in the process.

"You mean there's actually a place *worse* than this?" Derek asked.

"Oh, yes. The Abyss is the ultimate horror of horrors. It's a place with no light, no sound, no *anything*. And that's just for starters. From what I'm told, once you're in it, it sucks every ounce of time out of you. You actually go backwards to when you were an infant and then… pop!"

"Pop?!" Sam said with a look of sudden alarm.

"Pop! You just implode, and all that's left is the thought of you. And that thought can float in the Abyss for thousands of years until someone re-charges it with time. And as you might guess, there aren't too many volunteers down here who would donate their time to a mere dried-up thought of an Earthling."

Humphries paused as he looked about the cave.

"It's this way. I know it. Or at least I think I know it." He pawed at a clump of dangling moss, partly obscuring one of the exit tunnels; this one sat a couple of feet off the floor, about knee high in the wall.

"We'll have to lean in and slide face-first, belly side down. It's the only way. C'mon, follow me!" Humphries instructed and then abruptly stuck his head into the wall, wiggled his thick torso back and forth, and disappeared down the shaft.

"Not again!" Derek moaned. "'Follow me!' he says. What is this? Some twisted version of Simon Sez? We were following him the last time!"

"If it gets us one step closer to some answers, I'm in," said Sam.

"Let me go first, Sam, who knows what's down there," Max cautioned. "Derek, pull up the rear, and watch for anything suspicious."

"Suspicious?" Derek complained. "Are you kidding? What's *not* suspicious around here… Hey! Wait up!" Derek yelled, diving in headfirst after them.

Max was already committed. No matter where the slippery shaft ended, he would just have to just deal with it, in real time.

What I would give to hear some good news, he thought to himself.

But all he heard instead was a scream.

CHAPTER 15

"**G**et 'em off me!"

Humphries' eyes were frantic with fear. Attached to each one of his six arms were dozens of small prickly creatures with bulbous eyes and sharp yellow teeth. Some were biting, some tugging, all were excreting a thick, gooey substance that smelled like spoiled milk. As they systematically went about their work, they gave out an eerie hum that rose and fell in unison.

"Don't just stand there!" Humphries screamed. "Use the Extractor!" He motioned helplessly toward the apparatus in Max's hands. Max snapped out of his stupor and looked down at the flashing buttons.

"The blue one... point it and push the blue one," begged Humphries.

No sooner were the words out of his mouth when several of the humming, drooling needle-balls turned their attention toward the Extractor in Max's hands and lunged at it. Max instinctively hit the blue button, and a jagged bolt of blue neon light struck the lead creature head-on. The shockwave sent it reeling backwards, letting out a horrible shriek. Immediately, the other creatures scattered in panic as their leader shriveled to what resembled a dusty, old prune. Their docile humming was now replaced with loud yakking as they disappeared into the darkness. Humphries lay motionless, eyes rolled back in his head.

"Humphries, are you okay?" Max asked.

Silence.

"Derek—quick—grab his three arms on your side and I'll grab the other three. Maybe if we get him in a sitting position, he'll be able to breathe. C'mon, hurry!"

"'Breathe'?" Humphries drawled with disdain, his eyes still firmly shut. "For your information, Boggarts don't breathe. We *ventilate*. But thank you very much for trying. No, I was just allowing myself time to regenerate. Those hobgoblins took quite a few chomps out of me."

As Max and Derek looked at Humphries' arms, they could see chunks of flesh missing—bite marks that were miraculously healing before their eyes.

"That is way cool!" Derek shouted. "If I could do that, I'd try every daredevil skateboard trick in the book, like a McTwist or a 720 on a half-pipe… Heck, I could go for a 900—"

"Not so fast," Humphries interrupted. "It uses up a lot of life force to do this. And I'm on a budget, as you may recall."

"But why did those things attack you?" Sam asked. "Aren't they on your side?"

"No one is on anyone's 'side' down here except by force. And just try making nice with a hobgoblin. They're renegades and pirates, actually more like bank robbers, that attack Boggarts like me."

"But why?" Max asked.

"They are at the bottom of the food chain, the last to get any prana. So, some go feral like wild dogs. They work in groups and usually attack a single Boggart at a time. I normally travel with a changeling, but I lost my protection when I went to jail. You see Max, changelings can—"

"Yeah, I know," Max said, eyes rolling "I'm well aware…"

Undeterred, Humphries continued, "And despite being so small, those hobgoblins are not scared of anything, like little pit bulls. Well, except for Abaddon, of course."

"Abaddon! Abaddon! What is your deal with this guy, Humprhies? I think you're obsessed," Derek said shaking his head, as he bent over to touch the gooey drool left by one of the hobgoblins. "Man, this stuff is truly gross," he said, pulling up a long, wet strand of the substance from the cave floor. Here, Sam, touch it," he said, holding it up near her face.

"What is it with you and all things gross, Derek!" Sam demanded.

"Forget about it," sighed Humphries. "None of this matters anyway if you don't get to the Vault before The Transformation."

"That's when it all happens, doesn't it?" Max asked. "When they all drink all the contents, the prana from the Time Vault and enter our world, right?"

Humphries nodded. "Some of you Earthies call it Armageddon."

"Armageddon!!" both Derek and Sam exclaimed at the same time, looking at each other in disbelief.

"Wait, wasn't that a movie once?" Derek asked, racking his brain.

"And it's going to happen when the Vault reaches five hundred billion years, right?" Max continued, pressing Humphries for everything he knew.

"Hmmmm…" said Humphries, tapping the tip of his wrinkled nose with two of his lengthy forefingers. "Only Abaddon knows that for sure, but that would actually be a very good guess, Max. Lemme see," he continued calculating in his head. "Five hundred billion years of stored Vault time divided by the average human lifespan of say more or less seventy years, would equal a little over seven billion human lifetimes… yes! Five hundred billion years of shall we say 'tank time' would be enough to surpass the total current lifetimes on Earth. That would definitely tip the balance."

"So then, how close are we to that number?" Sam inquired, snapping her fingers to get Humphries' attention as he continued mumbling formulas and rechecking his math.

"Oh, uh, yeah! I'd say close, very close. Judging by the constant stream of Boggarts I've seen coming and going lately, it shouldn't be much longer at all. During your so-called Dark Ages, we tried to break through to your world with about a hundred million lifetimes and, to be perfectly honest, it just wasn't enough. All it did was start plagues and famine and disease. Very messy. I think we can agree that everyone lost out on that one. But that's not going to happen this time; Abaddon's made sure of that." With that, Humphries pushed himself up and headed toward yet another tunnel entrance. "If you don't mind, I'd like to get going before we run into something *really* nasty."

"Nastier than those hobgoblins?" Derek asked incredulously.

"Oh, yes! Those bug biters are really quite harmless compared to wereboars."

"Wereboars. Uh-huh, okay…" Derek muttered while stepping up and down in a vain attempt to remove the hobgoblin goo stuck to the bottoms of his shoes.

"Trust me on that one. I'd take a gaggle of hobgoblins over a herd of wereboars any day. Unless, of course, you enjoy being shocked by high-voltage tusks and trampled into cave dust." Humphries paused and shook his head for a moment. "I swear, they never paid me enough for this job. It's the underworld equivalent of being a postal worker."

"Well," Max said, "if we can empty the Time Vault and stop this Abaddon, maybe you can go find another line of work."

Humphries halted in his tracks.

"Stop Abaddon?" He turned toward Max and raised his unibrow in disbelief. "The Vault is one thing, but the best way to deal with Abaddon is to completely avoid him—at all costs." Humphries shuddered again, a habitual tendency whenever he got nervous. "I've seen Abaddon extract every ounce of time out of a whole legion of Boggarts, and then bottle up their shriveled remains in a tiny, corked bottle and toss it into the Abyss… ruined everyone's mojo for a month."

"Why would he do that to his own workers?" Sam exclaimed, as if trying to assemble a puzzle with missing pieces.

"They were forty-three seconds behind schedule, and he wanted to make an example out of them. I guess he figured the rest of the Boggarts would work all the faster."

"Sounds like a lousy boss," said Derek.

"Yeah, you could say that. But if it's the Vault you're after, I can get you there, but I would most definitely leave Abaddon alone."

"Well, it's not just the Vault he's after," Derek stated. "He's—"

"Derek!"

"What Sam? I'm just sayin'…"

"But *he* doesn't have to know," Sam replied, giving Derek the stink eye.

"What?" Humphries said, using all three of his own eyes to stare at each one of them. "Oh, we're keeping secrets now, are we?"

Max paused and took in a breath.

"I was told someone else might have made their way down here besides the monks—someone more recently."

"Really?" Humphries inquired with great interest. "Pray, tell who? Remember I've been in jail, so I'm not all that current."

"His dad," Derek stated, shooting a glance back at Sam.

"Your father?" Humphries replied, gathering up his large brow. "Well, that would explain—"

"Explain what?" Max shot back. "So, you do know something?"

"No, not at all, it's just that there was *a lot* of chatter lately, and a command to hurry things up, as if there was some threat to the system. A bit like the stir that you three have caused."

"So, he *could* be here?" Max said, eyes wide and leaning in toward Humphries.

"Can't say for sure, but if he is, they could be keeping him for questioning."

"Where?"

"Quandary," Humphries stated. "And if you think my prison was bad, at least I was conscious."

"So, just where is this—"

"Wait!" Humphries interrupted, putting several fingers in the air. "Did you hear that?"

"Hear what?" asked Derek.

Suddenly, a harsh grunting sound echoed from one of the tunnels, bouncing off the walls.

"Wereboars! Quick—this way!"

CHAPTER 16

H umphries took off like a shot.

"Let's go!" Max shouted, motioning to Derek and Sam. "We can't afford to lose him." Max scooped up the Extractor and took off after Humphries, with Derek and Sam close behind. They swerved down one narrow corridor before turning abruptly down the next, all the while half-running, half-falling with every step.

"Can you see him?" Derek shouted ahead to Max.

"No, not yet, but I see some of his tracks," Max yelled back. "Just make sure Sam is right behind you!" Max commanded.

Tunnel openings appeared two and then three at a time. Humphries zigged down one then zagged down another.

"Geez! Wait up, Humphries!" Max shouted to no avail. At each turn, he could hear the sound of hooves and wild grunting noises growing louder behind them, electric light from their shining tusks bouncing off the wall. Rounding a bend, Max spotted Humphries.

"They're gaining on us!" Humphries screamed, now running in a way Max hadn't seen before—galloping with all six arms and legs in rapid rotation like a windmill. Just as Max was catching up, Humphries dodged around a corner, then dropped from sight, seemingly into thin air.

Max slid to an abrupt stop, realizing the tunnel had led them back to the huge, cavernous main chamber—but now *above* it, far above it. He peered down toward his feet, realizing his toes now hung over a ledge perched a thousand feet above the main chamber floor.

WHAM!!

WHAM!! WHAM!!

Derek and Sam came slamming into Max's backside, sending him falling forward, arms flailing as his top half began to fall.

"Derek! Grab him!" Sam yelled.

"Gotcha!" Derek said, grabbing Max by his Extractor belt and hosting him back. But there was no time for thanks. The pounding of wereboar hooves echoed right behind them.

"Humphries! Where are you?" Max shouted.

"Down here!" came a voice.

Max looked down and saw nothing but long green fingers, all thirty of them. Humphries was dangling off the ledge, and he appeared to be in no rush to climb back up.

"Hurry!" he cried in a tremulous voice. "Jump off and grab hold of my back."

"Do what?!" Derek exclaimed.

"We don't have a choice!" Max said, now giving Derek a shove. "Sam, gimme your hand!"

Max, Derek, and Sam locked gazes as they spiraled off the ledge and through space, fear reflecting in their eyes. In that slow motion moment, they could smell the putrid breath of the wereboars, galloping at breakneck speed, horns down and flashing for the attack. Just as the hoofed beasts tilted their heads to gore the three, they also disappeared over the ledge, clutching desperately to grab hold of Humphries' slick back. Derek managed to catch hold of one of Humphries' arms, but Max missed and went sliding off before latching onto one of Humphries' feet, Sam now dangling below him by a hand. The wereboars, fully committed to the assault, could no longer stop their large bodies from sailing off the ledge overhead, shrieking and thrashing about as they plummeted. Max, Derek, and Sam gazed down in horror as they disappeared like tiny black dots, their electric tusks flickering in the distance.

"Humphries! I'm slipping!" screamed Derek.

Before Humphries could make a move, Derek frantically clawed his way onto his back, locking his arms securely around his neck.

"Max, hang on!" Humphries yelled down, his voice hoarse from Derek's death-grip and his own long fingers slowly slipping from the ledge.

"Humphries! What do we do?" Max yelled, one arm wrapped desperately around Humphries' knobby legs, his other hand locked around Sam's hand and wrist in a death grip.

"What do *we* do? I'm the one being stretched apart and strangled!" Humphries yelled back.

"Wait!" Max shouted eagerly. "There's another cave ledge right below us. Can you swing us back and forth and drop us on it?"

"H-h-how far is it?" Humphries gasped.

"About eight feet."

"Do I have another choice?"

"No! So, start swinging!"

Humphries began slowly swinging his body weight forward and backward to gain some momentum. As he swung forward the third time, a chunk of the ledge above them broke off, and the three tumbled into space.

"Sam, drop on the count of three!" Max yelled down to her. "One, two…"

Sam was not waiting. She flung herself with all her might and came crashing down, rolling across the ledge until she hit the back wall. Max fell right behind her, with Humphries and Derek landing on top of him. Despite the scrapes and bruises, all three lay there relieved, thankful for the firm, rocky outcropping.

"That was close," Max sighed after a long pause.

"Too close," Sam agreed. "This is turning out to be way harder than any of us thought."

"Hey! A bit of help here," Humphries gasped in a hoarse cry, pointing to Derek's fingers still gripped around his throat.

"Derek… Derek!! You can let go now," Max instructed, giving Derek a nudge.

Derek opened his eyes and blinked a moment. Seeing he was finally safe, he released his stranglehold on Humphries and rolled onto the rock slab. "Nice job, Max!" he said. "No thanks to ol' three-eyes here. You could have told us the tunnel came to a dead end."

Humphries ignored Derek's ingratitude and pointed down to the main chamber floor. "If you want to see where we're going, there it is."

Both Max and Derek sat upright. "Where?"

"Just beyond that bit of bubbling lava over there. See the large black area with the glowing light in front of it?"

"That's the Vault?" asked Max.

"In all its glory… capable of holding all of humanity's lifeforce and condensing it down to nothing more than an oversized jug of thick syrup."

"Syrup," Derek sighed. "I could go for some pancakes right about now…"

"Syrup that any army from either side of our worlds would fight and die for."

"I'd rather no one get the chance," Max said. "Come on, Humphries, *think*. There's got to be a better way to get down there. Unless we just head back into the tunnels?"

"Yeah," Derek interjected. "Isn't there some kind of zipline or something we could just take there?"

"Oh! Yes, by all means, I must have forgotten," Humphries replied sarcastically, using all six hands to smack his forehead. "It goes straight to the Vault, and there's a big sign there with a kill switch you can kick as you go by, and then take the escalator out of here. Abaddon will gladly validate your parking ticket."

"No need to get snippy!" Sam said. "We're just trying to figure it out and you're the only one that knows this place."

"Well, not necessarily," said Max, now rummaging through his backpack. "I recall seeing something that looked very similar to what's down there." With that, Max pulled out the worn leather manuscript and, flipping quickly through it, placed it face up in between them all.

"You mean you have it—the manuscript—on you!!" Humphries blurted out loud, backing up and almost falling off the ledge a second time.

"Yes, yes, in fact, I do, so what?" Max replied.

"That is one hot ticket, young man—wowzer, a real collector's item. Can I see it?"

"Don't trust him, Max," Derek warned.

"Hey, you three found *me*, remember? Locked up in prison? I'm no fan of this place or its management. I just want to look it over; I've heard so much about it."

Max spun the manuscript around, revealing a detailed drawing, very much resembling the layout of the chamber floor below. On it, were marked various geometric shapes, some circles, some triangles, rectangles and boxes, numerous measurements, dotted lines, and a legend with small cryptic symbols that Max had never seen before.

"Impressive, I must admit," Humprhies said, pouring over the drawing. "And it's done almost to scale." Humphries looked up at Max. "Where did you say you got this?"

"It's not important," Max said. "What *is* important is we find a way down here, and it looks like this marks a clear path," he said, pointing to the dotted line, which began at the rear of the chamber floor and led through a series of twists and turns, inside a walled gate and then to a triangle with an X marking a spot.

"Like I said, it does appear to be pretty spot on, I'll give you that. There's the Vault, the map shows it right where the X is. But seeing the layout and getting there are two very different things. You can't just waltz right in."

"Why not?" Derek demanded.

"First, there's the more immediate issue of getting down to the rear chamber floor from this ledge." Humphries then took a long finger and traced the dotted line. "Then we have to pass through the valley of voices, get by the outer security wall, avoid the guard towers, and if by some miracle we make it, get to the Vault itself."

"You're forgetting one other stop," Max said, looking Humprhies straight in the eyes.

"What? Like that's not enough?"

"Quandary, you said that's where they kept people for questioning, where is that at?"

"Max," Humphries sighed. "You've got no shot at this in the first place, it's a fool's errand, and while I've grown really attached to you three, you in particular seem intent on making this a suicide mission."

"I didn't come all the way down here to leave without answers… not just the Vault, I want to know about my dad, if he's here, if not, what happened to him." Max's voice trembled with tension, his eyes brimming for a moment.

Derek and Sam pulled in tight behind Max, as if forming a wall of their own. "Yeah, we're in this to see it through," Sam said.

"Darn right," Derek agreed.

"Alright, suit yourselves. I'm just saying, Quandary is not what you think it is, Max. They call it that for a reason."

"Well, the only reason I'm wondering about right now is why we ever unlocked you in the first place," Derek stated flatly.

"He's right, Humphries, the deal was to find a way to get down there, remember?" Max said, pointing repeatedly to the chamber floor below. "This ledge is not exactly The Gates of Ishtar."

"Hmmm... yes, yes, of course, what to do, what to do..." Humphries said, thinking hard. "I haven't traveled these back tunnels in eons—seems they've rerouted a few things. I don't think the tunnels are the best way to go."

"You think?" Sam agreed, gesturing as she picked out small chunks of dried cave residue still embedded in her hair, clothes, and shoes.

"Agreed," Derek said with a shake of his head. "I'm so over crawling though these tunnels. I'm beginning to feel like a human earthworm."

"An earthworm! Derek! Where do you come up with these marvelous ideas?"

Derek blinked at him in amazement. "Who, me?"

"It's brilliant!" Max shouted excitedly, his voice echoing to the depths of the chamber floor. "We need to convince someone or something to bring us down there, and you may just be the bait we need!"

CHAPTER 17

"**Y**eah, right," Derek said, "I'm going to play dead so you three can hitch a ride on the back of a Nark?" He turned his back on Max, Sam, and Humphries in a show of disgust, arms folded defiantly across his chest, and felt the lip of the sheer ledge under his feet. Loose rocks tumbled into the darkness below.

"It's actually not the worst idea," Sam said, "and it might be our only chance to get down there. Besides, Humphries said Narks only carry people off—they don't eat them, right?"

"She's 100% correct," agreed Humphries. "I've never known them to actually eat anyone. It's against company rules. They can only take you to the Tribunal, no snacking along the way. Mauling, perhaps, but not eating."

Derek continued in amazement. "Max, do you hear this? And let's say I don't get eaten, and we just get hauled to some, what was it, Tribunal? Put in some torture chamber to await our trial before getting thrown into the Abyss. I usually like your thinking, Max, but this time I think I'll wait for Plan B."

"I have to admit, he's really not all that far off, Max," Humphries chimed in. "And I'm not a big fan of Narks myself."

"You're no help, Hump. C'mon, just stay with me on this, all of you." Max paused a second, looked over at Sam, raising his eyebrows as if to say *help me out on this!*

"Yeah!" Sam interjected. "Derek, you can lay on the ground like you're wounded, that's what usually attracts prey. A Nark sees you, and while it swoops down, Humphries can jump on first, he's got more hands than all of us. Once he's on, he'll grab hold of Max and me, pull us aboard and we'll head out."

"Again, admire the thinking," Humprhies said, "remarkable really. I like the way you fleshies think, but a Nark isn't just going to simply drop us off and let us go. They aren't joyrides—they're messengers of death. A ride on a Nark is always a one-way ride that ends in the Abyss."

"Not if we use this!" Max grinned, holding up the Time Extractor.

"What?" Both Derek and Humphries glared at Max.

"Shoot a Nark in midair with that and you'll fall straight to the chamber floor," Humphries stated matter-of-factly. "You'll have Imps shoveling you up in minutes and using you for Wereboar food."

"Not if we time it right," Max insisted. "We'll zap the Nark just before landing, then run for cover and hide. From there, on the back side of the Chamber, we can make our way across the Chamber floor using the map in the manuscript, everything is laid out. We'll cross through, look for my dad, then find the Vault. How hard can that be?"

Derek and Humphries eyed each other nervously.

Sam nodded, "Let's do it."

"It might be a long shot, but I guess it's our only shot," Derek agreed reluctantly.

"I hate narks," Humphries said, "did I mention that?"

Max sighed with relief.

"One last question," Derek said. "Why do *I* have to be the bait? I don't recall volunteering."

"You *were* the one who came up with the earthworm idea," Humphries admitted, "just saying."

"Hey! Keep outta this!" Derek shot back.

"I need to get an overview of the layout of this place from the air and to make sure we're hearing in the right spot. Plus, someone has to man the Extractor, to hit the Nark at just the right time."

Derek leaned against a stone outcropping and slowly slid his back down until he was seated cross-legged. "I guess there's not much choice. So, what do I do, lay there with a sign on me that says, 'Eat Me'?"

"Not unless you *want* to be eaten," Sam insisted. "Derek, just lay there, it's not that big a deal. And remember, they won't eat you, because it's their job to remove things that don't belong. So maybe you could just, you know, moan real loud—right, Humphries?"

"Moaning is good," Humphries said with a nod. "I could use my fingernails to add a few bleeding cuts around your head and neck, that might help."

Max shot him a look. "No, that won't be necessary. Moaning should do it."

"We'll be right inside the tunnel opening," Sam instructed Derek. "As soon as one swoops down, Humphries jumps first, then Max and I."

"Don't worry Derek, this will all work out."

"I swear to God, you're going to owe me big time, Max. If we ever get out, all my homework for next year and *real* junk food at your house—no nutrition bars, soy milk, or any of that crap."

"Deal."

Max clutched the Time Extractor tightly and tucked back into the mouth of the cave, huddling down low behind Humphries, Sam just to his back. Derek dutifully positioned himself, lying down near the lip of the cave ledge. The three anxiously waited, just inside the cave's dark shadow, peering out just enough to get a view of Derek without being seen.

Minutes passed without a sound.

"Maybe moan a little bit louder," Sam whispered hoarsely.

"Really? I'm getting hungry laying here," Derek whined. "This ledge smells like my grandma's okra, which I could almost eat right now."

"Shhhh!" Max said. "I think something's coming!"

It was a faint flapping sound in the distance. As they listened, it grew louder and louder.

"Something's coming, all right," Humphries said grimly, "but from the wrong direction!"

Max and Sam whirled around and looked into the depths of the cave. Something was moving in the dark, something glistening, slithering, hissing. Panic washed over him. *Easy, now,* he told himself. He recalled his father's calming words from long ago, when Max was afraid of the dark: "I'm right here Max, and just remember, whatever is out there, you can face it."

"You're here. I can face this." Max reassured himself. "Here goes nothing!"

Suddenly, out of the blackness appeared an enormous, yawning mouth lined with razor-sharp fangs.

"Leviathan!!" Humphries shouted. "Cave snakes! They scavenge the tunnels."

Sam jumped backwards, crashing into Max, knocking him and Humphries over like bowling pins back toward the ledge. The gigantic serpent emerged from the cave opening, its jaws widening and neck flared. With nowhere to run, Max, Sam, and Humphries all knelt down next to the out strewn Derek, hands covering their heads and necks to ward off the inevitable attack. The nostrils of the Leviathan shot a blast of hot air into their faces as its tongue slithered, feeling around the hard ledge surface, right between their squatted feet.

"They're blind, they're cave snakes!" Humphries whispered quietly to the huddled threesome. "So just don't move," he instructed.

"Any other ledges below us?" Max said to Humphries.

"No, this is it!"

The mouth of the oversized viper opened impossibly wider as it drew within inches of them, nostrils searching for any whiff, any vibration of them. They winced for fear of the pain. Then it happened.

Whoosh!

A violent blast of air knocked Max off his feet. But instead of razor teeth ripping into his body, he felt something clamping hard onto his arms. Max battled to keep his senses, but everything was reeling about him. *Have I just been eaten?* he wondered.

When he slowly opened his eyes, it was all gone. Everything. The cave. The giant Leviathan. Darkness surrounded him except for brief flashes of eerie light. The last time Max wondered if he had died was in the bookstore when the Changelings had hurled him against the wall. This time the pain was more intense, all in his arms, and it didn't stop.

Clear my thoughts! Clear my thoughts! he repeated to himself.

That's what Zadkiel had told him to do, and he was determined to do it. Gathering his strength, he focused harder. This time he made out what looked like two huge black claws, one wrapped securely around each of his arms. He glanced around to his left and right, spotting Sam, Derek, and Humphries, seemingly floating through the air.

Thank God! They're alive! I'm alive!

But relief quickly turned to stark terror as Max slowly recognized the outlines of three enormous Narks, their black claws clenching their prey.

Max tilted back his head to see the underbelly of a fourth Nark flapping strenuously above him. The vice-like grip of its talons dug in even deeper, his arms beginning to feel numb. Fear and dread flooded Max's mind. Moments ago, he had felt the indescribable relief of having narrowly escaped certain death, and now death seemed more certain than ever.

CHAPTER 18

Max peered down below. No wonder he felt his arms but not his feet! He was hanging suspended, soaring along, a thousand feet over the immense central cavern of Nemesis. Below were swarms of tiny, strange creatures, inhabitants of Nemesis, like ants from this distance, going dutifully about their tasks. Max wondered if this is what ancient Egypt looked like from above, workers busily building complex canal systems, giant-sized sphinxes, and grand pyramids, structures that rose high and mighty up toward the sky, ones that held the promise of eternity.

"Max, anytime would be great," Humphries shouted, hanging like a slowly dripping, gooey glob of Jello by two thin outstretched arms on the underside of an oversized Nark. "These big birds are going to make a wide turn at the back of the Chamber on their approach to the Tribunal. Unless you want a date with the abyss, I suggest we make a pit stop about now."

Max glanced down at the ground below them. Sure enough, the Narks were sweeping wide against the vast cavern wall at the back of the Chamber, casting an oversized shadow. Straining their thick muscular necks, they tilted their rough canvas-like wings at a sharp 45-degree angle, dropping lower and lower for the approach.

"But I can't reach the Extractor," Max shouted back, arms held apart by the powerful grip of the Nark's talons. "The plan was to be on *top* of these things."

"Just swing yourself!" Sam yelled back to him.

"What did you say?" Max yelled back, unable to hear above the din of the wind and flapping wings.

"Swing your weight back and forth, left and right, let the Extractor swing with you, then grab it with one hand!" she instructed.

Huh, Max thought, *great idea!* as he began thrusting his hips and legs to one side then the other. The Extractor swung closer, then closer, but still not quite in reach."

"Hurry. Max, they're making the turn!" Derek yelled.

"GOT IT!" Max said, grabbing hold of the Extractor with his right hand just above the trigger.

ZZZZAAAAPPPPP!

The first shot rang out, right into the soft underbelly of the Nark above him. The winged creature howled, raised up its head, and then instantly let go of Max, sending him spiraling toward the ground. Max landed in what looked like a row of thick twisted vines, breaking his fall, but he had no time to question anything. Tuning his Extractor skyward, he let out three quick volleys into the underbellies of the remaining three Narks.

AAARRRKK! AAARRRKK! AAARRRKK!

One by one, first Sam, then Derek, then Humphries, fell like rain, landing in the same thorny patch of brush.

"Is there nothing at all soft down here?" Derek complained, getting up and checking his head, neck, and hands for scratches.

"Hey, we're alive," Sam said. "It could be worse."

"Well… yes and no," Humphries said, working to get his overstretched arms back to their original lengths.

"What do you mean?" asked Max. "You said it was better to start back at the back of the cavern, away from all tight security around the Vault."

"The staffed security, the security with all the Barghests and Wereboars, but this back here has security of its own. We'll call it systemic security—it runs on its own."

"Really, how so?" Max asked, peering once again at the map of the floor plan of Nemesis. "It says we're right here, in the Valley of Voices, near this network of paths. These dots go straight ahead, then make a few twists and turns, and then go on to the Vault, near the center of Nemesis."

"Then go right ahead and lead the way, in fact, you're already right here"—Humphries pointed out on the map—"right at the entrance to the Maze of Madness."

"The what?" Derek shot up.

"What exact type of maze are we talking about?" Sam asked, now running her fingers along the dotted line as well, as if to memorize the turns.

"Just your typical left turn, right turn, that sort of thing," Humphries reassured them. "There's nothing to it, unless…"

"Okay, unless what?" Derek said, exasperated.

"Unless you have something on your mind, that's all."

"Everyone has something on their mind," Sam said, "that doesn't make any sense."

"Well then, my advice? Do not enter! These bushes have a way of messing with people who are preoccupied. Even with a clear mind and a clear goal, this maze is no cake walk. But if you are an overthinker, then you should think twice!"

"We'll have to just do our best," Max said. "We've gotta get through, and I'm not going to let a few bushes stop me." With that Max slipped the manuscript back into his backpack, swung the Extractor over his shoulder, and made his way toward the one opening in the row of thorny brush.

"Anyone care to join?" he asked as he began to enter.

"You might think twice about just who goes in first," Humprhies advised, "the Maze only affects the leader."

"Well, since I got you all involved in this, it's my job to get us through and out, that's on me." And with that, Max disappeared into the first row.

CHAPTER 19

"**H**uh… the Valley of Voices, the Maze of Madness—this stuff has a nice ring to it! I wonder who does the marketing down here?" Derek asked aloud, doing his best to avoid the sharp thorns that lined the tight rows of gnarled twisting stalks and vines. Max was well down the first path, its edges strangely cut and pruned back as if there was some underworld gardener in charge of the place.

"Sam, do me a favor and take out the manuscript. I think it would be best if you could look it over so I can keep my eyes peeled ahead," Max said as they approached the first turn.

"Sure thing," Sam replied, unsnapping the clasp and quickly flipping the book open, tracing their path turn by turn. "Up here, go left," she said, "in about fifty feet."

"Well, Max! Maxwell Kellerman! What a surprise seeing you here!"

Max had turned the corner to see, of all people, Ms. Stolty standing in front of him.

"Leave it to you, Max," she said, eyeing him from head to toe, holding her spectacles up to her eyes for close inspection. "Getting all your friends involved in some cockamamy, hare-brained scheme. It's enough that you don't pay attention in class and ruin things for yourself, but this is just too much. I blame this on myself really, I should have just made a referral on you, before you went and messed up everyone else's lives…"

"Ms. Stolty?"

"Ms. Stolty, what? Max, who are you talking to? Are you alright?" Derek shot back. "Keep moving, you're just standing there."

"You didn't see…?" Max turned back and no one was there. Looking side to side, he continued on, all the more cautious.

"Up ahead to the right," Sam instructed, "there's two right turns in a row."

Max rounded the corner, staying as close to the center as possible.

"Kellerman! How's the drooling problem coming along, finally got it under control?" a thunderous laugh followed.

"Kyle? Saunders?"

"Why did your parents ever even call you Max? They should have called you Minimum? Cause your brain's so small!"

"Wow, Kyle, that doesn't even make sense."

"You don't make sense, Max, that's why no one hangs out with you, except your little weirdo friends."

"I'd take my friends any day over—"

"MAX!" Sam yelled, breaking into Max's thoughts.

"What? Did you say something Sam?"

"No! You did. You're talking to someone, sounded like you said Kyle? Saunders?"

"C'mon," Max said, "I think I know why they call this the Maze of Madness. We need to get out of here."

With that, Max quickened his pace, racing to the next turn.

"Wait, Max, you won't know which way to go," Sam yelled, trying to keep up. Derek and Humphries followed in quick pursuit.

"Max! You're the only one I trusted, the one I gave everything I had to. It all depends on you…"

"Professor Gutt? No, it can't be, something's wrong."

"Max, stop!" shouted Sam at full volume. "Just stop!"

Max dropped to the ground, covering his ears.

"Max, whatever you're hearing, it's not you, it's not you, Max," Sam reassured him. "Let it go!"

"But I can't," Max said. "Even if it is this stupid maze, it's still true. I've gotten everyone involved, it's my fault. It's all a mess."

With ears covered and eyes closed, Max tried to block out the thoughts, but they just kept coming. As they did, he felt the touch of leaves brush across his pants. Opening his eyes, he saw the twisted vines, now alive with motion, wrapping themselves around him like a stealthy boa constrictor.

"Get off me!" Max yelled angrily, himself twisting and turning in response. The thick branches now encircled him completely, wrapping tightly around his forehead. Little, tiny shoots probing his ears and nostrils, as if looking for entry.

"Failure!" whispered the vines. "Nothing but failure. No reason to keep trying. You're a disappointment, Max."

"Tune it out, Max! Don't let it get to you," Sam cried. "There's nothing here!"

Tune it out, Max thought. *Go to a different wavelength—a different wavelength! Like theta waves!* Max took a deep breath, but instead of fighting to free himself, he relaxed, releasing every muscle in his tense body.

Breathe, he thought to himself. *Just breathe.*

As he did, he felt a subtle shift, something almost undetectable. The whispers faded. The loud voices, the ones yelling, lecturing, mocking, began to soften, retreat, and weaken. As he opened his eyes, the thick walls of vine around him shook for a moment, then began dropping their thorns. New leaves jutted out in every direction in a rich, vibrant green. Flowers began to bloom, each with a different aroma, a delicate fruit-like fragrance. Max paused to inhale again, this time taking in a full breath; the air smelled sweet, like it does after an early summer rain.

"Nice, isn't it?"

The tall, bearded giant appeared, sitting next to Max, arms outstretched, interlocking his fingers behind his head, elbows extended out, now leaning back against the lush sprouted bushes.

"Zadkiel!"

"So glad you dropped by, Max."

"Wait, I didn't drop by... you did."

"Did I, Max? I thought I wasn't allowed to be down here, remember?"

"Oh wait, you aren't, so how are you here?"

"Here is where I always am, Max. You were just able to find me, that's all, to tune in as they say. A broadcast tower broadcasts... the signal travels... the receiver receives."

"So, you're just what, then? In another dimension? Broadcasting remotely? Here, just in my mind?"

"That depends. To some degree, isn't everything in your mind, Max? What happened to all the voices you were just hearing?"

"They stopped."

"Hmmm, *you* didn't stop them… *they* just stopped by themselves. Interesting."

"Well, I guess it's how you think about it."

"Really? Well then, sounds to me like you're getting somewhere, Max," Zadkiel said with a slight smile. "And speaking of getting somewhere, you've got some business to attend to."

"So, wait! Empyrean, this place we're in right now, just tell me is it *real?*"

"Yes, Max, Empyrean is very much real, just as you imagined." And with that, Zadkiel was gone.

"Max, we gotta go!" came the voice.

"What? Where? I mean…"

Max tried to refocus. He looked down at his feet, then at his hands. The vines were gone, all back in their original place.

"You were yelling at someone… or something," Derek insisted. "Are you okay, man?"

"Yeah, yeah, I'm good," Max said, now looking up at both him and Sam. They both extended a hand, and Max was once again back on his feet. "What do you say we get out of this brain teaser?"

With that they were on their way again, Sam calling out several more lefts and rights. The vines seemed to whisper in the wind, but Max paid them no attention. He was focused on the way forward, the path ahead.

CHAPTER 20

"**B**rain teaser?"

Derek muttered under his breath as they exited the maze, checking himself for cuts. "That felt more like a head scratcher, and not the fun kind. Ow! Sam, can you pull this one out?"

Derek leaned forward, pointing to a part in his hair. Sam obliged, carefully removing the last remaining thistle lodged in his scalp.

"Well, that's what you get for cutting corners," she said, shaking her head.

"Yeah, yeah, so where to now?" Derek asked. "'Cause I'm wondering if there's food along the way."

"Snack bars will have to suffice," Max said, tossing each of them what was left of his remaining stash in the backpack.

"Blueberry almond? Really?" he complained, half the bar already stuffed in his mouth.

"Looks like we're about halfway to the Vault," Sam said, still examining the map from the manuscript. Max pulled alongside Sam.

"What do you know about where we're at, Humphries?" Max asked, looking around for their three-eyed host. "Humphries?"

Humphries sat quietly on the ground near the exit from the maze, picking small pebbles out from between his toes, then tossing them mindlessly back into the thorny brush. "I hesitate to say anything, Max," he replied coolly.

"Why's that?" Max countered.

"Because it only gets worse from here, don't you get it? Remember all these contraptions, these systems, were created to keep fleshies like you out of this place. They were designed to protect the Vault; the inhabitants of Nemesis, they are no bueno for your types."

"Aww! Humphries! You're getting attached to us, aren't you?" Sam declared, plopping down next to him and giving his enormous thick neck a big squeeze.

Humphries bristled, sitting back up straight. "No, that's silly, ridiculous!" He shuddered briefly, running through a quick change of colors, flashed a fiery bright red before returning to his original slimy green-gray self. "It's really just a simple question of self-preservation. Why should I risk my neck if you're just going to do yourselves in anyway?"

"Regardless, Humphries, you know we can't turn back, so just spill the beans, what's the bad news?" Max insisted. "What's this thing ahead of us?" Max pointed to a large castle-like wall made of rough blocks of hewn stone, boulder-sized stone that appeared to have been there for millennia.

"That's the Threshold, the outer wall that protects Nemesis central, basically your version of downtown, and it's the highest security zone you'll find anywhere—Barghests, Narks, the whole gamut patrols central Nemesis. Inside is the nerve center, all the operations, the Tribunal, Quandary, The Vault…"

"Quandary? Did you say Quandary?"

"Yes, in fact, I just did, and I already wish I hadn't," Humphries said to himself, rolling all eyes skyward.

"Well then how do we get past this wall? We're wasting time!"

"To get through the Threshold you have to pass the Point of Paradox, which is ironic really, since no one knows how to pass the Point of Paradox."

"But there's a bridge right here!" Sam exclaimed, holding up the map for Humphries to see. "It goes straight across this zig zag line right up to a gate door in the wall."

"Hmmm," Humphries said wagging all six fingers on his top right hand. "Well, for starters, that zig zag line is a *fault* line, a big ol' crack in the floor of Nemesis, one that goes down a ways to some fairly unfriendly terrain. And the bridge itself is blocked by a stone."

"A stone? As in a rock? So?"

"Not just any stone, the Paradox Stone, it's very good at its job."

At that point the foursome had trudged forward, drawing closer to the objects on the map. In the near distance, a small clap of what sounded like thunder could be heard echoing up from the crack in the Chamber floor. Edging up to the fault, the three of them peered over its rim and down into the deep divide while Humphries stood back.

"Yikes!" exclaimed Derek. "You ain't kidding, the canyon down there looks like it could have its own weather system!"

"That's just it, it does," said Humphries, pointing at what looked like small dark clouds floating in at the top of the fault, right in front of them, flashing every few seconds with what appeared to be small bursts of energy, like tiny lightening skipping from one tiny cloud to the next. Each time the light flickered, a small rumble sounded, echoing down the deep, dark canyon walls to the unseen below.

"So obviously, that's *not* an option," Sam said. Then, spying the narrow bridge she had seen on the map moments before, she turned to the others. "Look over there, that's it!"

Moving to their right, they walked to the entrance of the narrow bridge. It looked to be made of a slick, smooth granite-like surface with no handrails or guards of any type except for a slight ridge, about a three-inch-high lip, on each of its sides. Blocking the way, about five feet out from the entrance of the bridge, sat a perfectly round stone, matching in color and appearance to that of the bridge, perched there like an oversized marble.

"That's it? That's the mysterious Paradox Stone?" asked a bewildered Derek. "How hard would that be to just move out of the way?"

"Careful, Derek!" Max cautioned. "They call it Paradox for a reason, so let's not be too quick to—"

"Max, look!" Sam was pointing to a small pile of rocks and other debris by the foot of the bridge. "Bones!"

Max, Sam, and now Humphries, drew closer to take a look. "They appear to be human," Humphries surmised.

"Max, you don't think it could have been your—"

"Look! See! It budged!" Derek had already thrust himself at the oversized stone at the entrance to the bridge, putting his shoulder into it to clear a path. "C'mon, help me and we can all move it across—it's just a matter of having enough people. It takes a group effort, that's the catch! That's the Paradox!" Derek said, proud that he had solved the mystery.

"Alright, alright!" Max replied. "Hold on. C'mon, Humphries, you've got lots of hands, get in here. Sam, push against my back while I push."

Derek leaned in harder, gripping his feet as best he could on the smooth bridge surface. The others piled in tight, each huffing and straining to dislodge the glossy stone.

"The ridges are keeping it from falling off; the only way is to keep pushing it forward in front of us, all the way across to the other side," Max yelled from his vantage point. Exerting force with all their might, Humphries pushing on top, Derek and Max in the middle, they inched their way forward, until the stone had been rolled about halfway across the dangerous divide.

"Don't look down," Max cautioned, as he eyed the darkness of the yawning canyon below. "Just keep pushing!" As they did, ripples of thunder sounded, now growing louder, the dark clouds floating, flashing, just off the bridge to the right and left of them.

And then something changed.

The bridge on which they were standing began to tilt slightly, ever so slightly upwards, creating gravity that pushed the giant marble back against the group.

"Hey! C'mon everybody, push!" yelled Derek. "I feel like I'm doing this all by myself!"

"We are pushing!" shouted Sam, distraught. "But the bridge is tilting up—the stone is beginning to roll backwards!"

"No! It can't," yelled Max, now frantically heaving himself against the weight of the marble ball. "Derek, c'mon… Humphries, push!"

But it was too late. The sheer weight of the smooth stone made it nearly impossible to stop, as both Max and Derek found their feet slipping. Humphries, unable to maintain his grip, slipped awkwardly and fell back a few feet behind the group.

"Lock your knees!" Max instructed, and Derek immediately did so. As they did, the ball continued its return, Max and Derek now skidding straight-legged backwards, Sam locked-kneed behind them.

"It's about to roll over you. You're going to get crushed!" warned Sam. "Humphries, help! Do something!!"

With no time to spare, Humphries, while still sitting, shot each set of three hands forward, like outstretched elastic bands, fingers twisting and straining to reach the pair.

"Gotcha!" he said, hands grabbing the back of each of their shirts, and snatching them back to where he was seated. The large marble stone was now rolling backwards full speed, now with Sam in its path.

"Run, Sam!" Max yelled, as he, Derek and Humphries retreated back across the bridge. Running to catch up, Sam could hear the thunderous roll of the weighty stone right behind her.

"Jump!" Max commanded.

Sam leapt off the bridge at the last second, grasping the canyon edge, feet dangling in space.

"Here, grab my hand!" Max shouted.

Sam grabbed hold and tried to hang on. "I can't, I'm slipping," she cried out, eyes wide with fear.

WHACK!

The suction-like grip of Humphries web hand, wrapped around her entire left arm, lifting her skyward and back on firm ground.

Once again, the crew found themselves laid out flat on their backs, speechless, breathing heavily as they lay staring blankly upward.

"Thank you, Humphries," Max finally said, letting out a deep sigh.

"Yeah, thank you both," Sam replied, equally grateful. "You too, Derek."

"Me? Hey, it's my fault, I shouldn't have just started pushing that thing in the first place."

"Did I mention that it was a Paradox?" Humphries finally said.

"Yes, yes you did," Max said, "but why didn't you just tell us the stone did that?"

"That's just it, Max, a Paradox, and it changes every time you come here. You never know what the particular challenge will be, only that it will be one."

"A paradox, hmmm…" Max mused, now getting back up on his feet.

"What are you thinking, Max?" Sam asked, seeing the wheels turning in his head.

"Paradox, irony, something counter intuitive, right?"

"Yes, from what I understand, sounds about right, why?"

"The Paradox Stone, it's about as hard as they come, correct?"

"Yeah?" Derek said, following along, not quite sure what paradox even meant.

"Well, what's the opposite of hard?"

"Hard as in?" Sam asked.

"Don't overthink it, just what's the opposite?"

"Easy?" offered Derek.

"Yes!" Max exclaimed. "And what else?"

"Soft??" Sam chimed in.

"Now we're getting somewhere!" Max said with delight.

"The Stone! The Rock! It's hard and difficult!"

"You can say that again," Derek said, rubbing his shoulders.

"The paradox is that it can be soft and easy!"

"What in the world are you talking about Max?" Sam exclaimed with growing exasperation.

"The clouds! They're soft, they're easy. They're steppingstones!"

With that, all eyes turned to the small floating puffs of dark, billowing clouds swaying like cottontails in the air rising from the canyon below. There they sat, just to the right and left of the bridge, slowly drifting back and forth.

"Are you crazy?" Derek exclaimed. "That's madness."

"Yeah, Max, how would you even test out your theory? The nearest cloud is about five feet from the edge."

"Ever hear of the leap of faith?" Max asked, now approaching the edge.

"No! No way! You're not thinking what I think you're thinking. That would be pure insanity."

"No, it wouldn't," Max replied, taking a running leap, "that would be Paradox." Just then, Max backed up, took a short run, and sprung, pushing off with both feet, flying through the air.

"MMMAAAXXX!!" shouted both Derek and Sam.

Max felt himself flying upward, a rush of exhilaration filled every cell of his body, until looking down, he saw the yawning cavity below. As his feet hit the pillowing surface of the cloud, he felt it give, as if he was passing right through it and down to certain death. But the cloud held, like a springing mattress; it gave a bit and then bounced back.

"Hey! See! It worked!" Max shouted, giving a little up and down victory dance on the dark billowy pillow.

"OMG, MAX!!" Sam screamed at him. "You freakin' scared the living daylights out of us. That is NOT funny!"

"Funny?" Max said, slowing down his bounce. "Wow, I was only—"

"Whatever," Sam replied, shaking her head.

"Hey," Derek shouted. "For the record, I think it was awesome!"

Max turned and looked ahead, stretching his leg out and placing his foot on the cloud next to him.

"Yep! Steppingstones," he said, now jumping from one to the next, each tiny cloud lighting up with small flashes of light as he made his way across. "C'mon, follow me, we got business to attend to!" his voice echoing down to the canyon below.

"Go on ahead," Humprhies motioned to Derek and Sam, "get across before me in case I pop one of those clouds," he stated, pointing ahead and then to his oversized belly.

Sam went next, gingerly jumping from cloud to cloud, trying not to look down. Derek followed, using every leap as an opportunity to see how high he could bounce. Humphries pulled up the rear, the floating clouds sinking down a foot or two every time he landed on one but holding firm still the same.

"There! We made it!" Max announced with a degree of satisfaction. There, in front of them, stood a towering set of large, wooden doors reaching up some thirty feet tall, each clad with iron hardware, as if crafted by medieval woodworkers from a bygone era.

"I wouldn't quite say 'made it'," Humphries cautioned.

"Why?" Sam inquired. "We just need to get through that door and—"

"And that's where the real trouble begins," Humphries warned. "Everything up till now has been systems, no one around. Once you cross The Threshold, it changes, full-time patrols, security everywhere."

"We'll just have to be extra careful," Max stated, as he pulled on a large latch that slowly opened the huge gates.

But it was already too late.

CHAPTER 21

"**G**rab them!" commanded the voice. "All of them!" Before Max could barely move, he felt hands all over him, knocking him and all the others forcefully to the ground. "Don't let them make a move!" the commands continued.

"What the heck!" Derek yelled, as he attempted to fight back against the throng of muscle-bound creatures surrounding them. The assailants stood upright on two feet but had the appearance of thick-skinned rhinos with large tusk-like horns for noses, with large black eyes protruding on each side. The brutish figures came equipped with armor, long shiny swords and metal tipped spears, using them to poke and prod their victims.

"Barghests!" Humphries said in disgust, spitting a string of gooey green slime at their feet.

WHACK! The head Barghest slapped Humphries upside the head. "You! Of all creatures, smuggling in the likes of these!"

Now bound by hands and feet, Max looked more closely at his latest captors. They had a strange reptilian quality to them, like something you would see in a bad sci-fi flick, scales running down their backs. Their large, chicken-like eyes rotated around in every direction, tracking their every move. Max made no attempt to struggle. This was not the time; he counted several dozen of them. The thorny-headed creatures went mechanically about the job of first binding then dragging them across a bumpy cobbled street, down two to three long blocks, to what appeared to be a holding facility, a police station of sorts, with a pair of griffins guarding the front of the entranceway.

"Book 'em!" the head Barghest yelled as they shoved the four to the ground in front of what must have been some sort of underworld magistrate, a thin, bug-looking creature, the walking stick kind, with narrow set eyes and tiny spectacles to help with its inspections.

"On what charge?" the official replied.

"Charges, as in plural," replied the head Barghest in a rough voice before listing them off.

"Violation of Airspace."

"Breaching the Threshold."

"Disrupting the Peace."

"The peace? Down here?" Derek muttered under his breath.

"SILENCE!" came the unexpected rebuke from the thin, wiry head of the magistrate.

"Anything else? Any other charges?" came the request.

"Yes, one final charge, for that one there," the Barghest insisted, pointing directly at Humphries.

"Treason!"

A shout went out around the room from the other Barghests, mixed with short grunting noises, and a stir of commotion.

"SILENCE!" the magistrate repeated.

"Put them in holding for now, the Tribunal will convene here shortly." With that, the stick-faced creature sounded a gavel, and the Barghest ushered Max, Sam, Derek and Humphries down a narrow stone corridor and placed them in a cell.

CLANK!

The metal door slammed shut behind them.

The four went tumbling towards the cold, hard ground, tossed there by the gruff guards.

"Great plan, Max, did I mention? And while you work the next one, could you make sure to include our funerals?"

"That's not his fault, Derek, and you know it," Sam injected. "We got ambushed. Something must have been watching us all along, a Nark perhaps, way up high."

"Hey," Max said. "All is not lost. We're still alive, aren't we? And we're closer than ever to the Vault, and to finally getting some answers."

"What we're really closest to?" Humphries volunteered. "The Tribunal! The other stuff is just wishful thinking."

"C'mon, Humphries, there must be some way out," Max said.

"Well, you would be the first to find it; although admittedly, you have found some success to this point. I'll give you that."

"Wait, so there was that magistrate, with all those weird underworld rules, is there someone or something we could appeal to?" Sam asked hopefully.

"Only Abaddon. And I don't think you'd like his idea of mercy."

"So what's the alternative, Humphries? Think! You know this place better than anyone."

"There's only one way I know out of here…"

"What's that?" Max and Derek asked, eyes lighting up.

"The Abyss."

CHAPTER 22

"**S**o how have you enjoyed your holiday so far?"

Max looked up to see Humphries resting comfortably against the prison wall, calmly filing the fourth fingernail of his fifth hand with a small flat rock he found on the prison floor.

"Oh, is that what they call death row humor, Humphries? Nice. Glad you aren't concerned at all."

"Hey! I don't want to be the one to say I told you so, but I absolutely told you so. It was only a matter of time for me, but you had a chance to get out, you, Library Mary there, and Boy Blunder, but you blew it."

Derek perked up. "You mean we could have gone back?"

"Anytime you wanted."

"But how?"

"What difference does it make now? You're locked up, and the Abyss is calling. Why live with regrets? That's my motto."

"I knew we could have gone back, Max! I swear, I'm never going to listen to either of you two for as long as I live."

"Don't worry there, Derek," Humphries said cheerfully, "that won't be for long,"

Derek lashed out at him. "As for you, three-eyes, I have a mind to go ahead and zap the living daylights out of you. If only we still had an Extractor. I'd just whip it right out now from this belt and buzz the living daylights out of—"

Max and Humphries sat up straight and locked their gaze on Derek.

"What? Why're you two lookin' at me like that? Do I have spinach in my teeth?"

Humphries could barely choke out the words. "You… you have the Boggart belt still on?"

Derek felt his shirt, patting it frantically with both hands, at waist level.

"Yeah! Yeah, it's right here, under my shirt, why?"

"WHY? Because it has every available Boggart tool in the kit," Humphries stated emphatically, as though it should not require an explanation, his face pulsating with shades of deep red and purple.

"Wow, I guess I should have said something?" Derek offered sheepishly.

"They must have never thought to check a fleshie for a Boggart belt," Humphries theorized. "Finally, a lucky break!"

"So, what does that mean, Humphries?" Max asked. "Can we use it when the guards come?"

"Let me think, let me think," he replied, once again tapping his fingers nervously as he took mental inventory. "It's actually more of a survival belt. All Boggarts wear them—it's standard issue. The key we used earlier to open my cell door would be great, but this one has a metal door, not bars, so that won't work. The Boggart whistle will only bring the guards, that's not a good idea. Wait! There is a BADD device on that belt."

"Bad?" they all asked in unison.

"Yeah, BADD, a Boggart Auto Destruct Detonator," he said. "Very powerful but it's only to be used in case of emergenc—"

"You mean this one?" Derek asked, holding up a flat rectangular box, the size of a phone charger. "And what does this little red button do?" he asked, giving it a push.

"NO! Not that button!" Humphries screeched, jumping to snatch the device out of Derek's hands. But it was too late. A shrill, ear-piercing alarm penetrated every corner of the jail cell. Armed guards could be heard running and shouting everywhere. Suddenly, several Barghests appeared at their cell door, beating on it furiously as one of them rifled desperately through a set of keys.

"What… what did I do?" Derek exclaimed with a bewildered look.

"You set it off!" Humphries shouted, eyes popping wide open, now stepping backwards toward Max.

"Set *what* off?"

"The detonator!"

"What does it detonate?"

"A Boggart! Like me! And everything within one hundred feet of one!"

As Max's and Derek's jaws dropped, the door opened with a click as one of the guards turned the key. What happened next was something that no one could have anticipated. In their panic to remove the auto-detonator before it wiped out the entire prison, the guards all shoved their way through the open door at the same time. The result was a chain-reaction pile-up, all five bulky bodies toppling across the floor like dominoes.

"Run!" Max yelled instinctively, pushing Sam ahead of him, then scrambling across the scaly backs of the fallen prison guards. Humphries followed closely behind with Derek in the rear. Derek leapt high, just high enough to clear the entire heap of Barghests, when the head prison guard reached up and snagged his shirt with his thick padded claw.

"Gotcha! You little fleshie!" the guard shouted.

"Hey!" Derek yelled back. "Looking for this?" and with that, he dropped the device right inside the Barghest's front armored plate, leaving him scrambling to pull it back out.

"C'mon!" Max yelled back at Derek. "Get outta there!"

Derek clambered out of there, while Max slammed the heavy metal door shut behind him.

"I can't lock it!" he called out to Derek and Humphries, pulling to get the door to click in place. "Sam, can you flip this latch?"

"Max, it's no use! The blast will kill us all," Humphries shouted from behind.

"Wait! Grab one of those Extractors there on the wall, Derek, then everyone huddle tight behind this door," he said, motioning them all to move in close. "Just grab on of one of these door rings and hold on tight—"

Kaboom! Before Max could get the next word out, a huge cracking sound came from inside the cell, blowing the roof clear off. It was followed by a blast of air that blew the huge prison door spiraling skyward, with Max, Sam, Derek, and Humphries gripping the edges, and each other, for dear life. The door reached higher and higher, all the while rotating slowly round and round, before beginning a gradual descent back toward the ground. The foursome soared, magic-carpet-style, over several buildings before landing abruptly on the back edge of the door, the front lip plowing up ground ahead of them before skidding to an abrupt stop. Max's ears were ringing from the blast.

"That… that…" Derek shouted between heavy pants of breath, "that was freaking awesome!!"

Humphries tugged at one of his hands, which was pinned beneath the prison door.

"C'mon, Derek, Sam! Off the door, we've got to lift this off Humphries and get out of here before those goons come looking for us."

"I'm afraid it's too late for that," Humphries said as the three strained to lift the heavy metal frame from off his flattened hand.

"Too late for what?" Max, Sam, and Derek gave the door a final heave that flipped the door over. "I mean it, if we don't get out of here now, those Barghests will find us, and we'll be hauled to the Tribunal."

"Max," Humphries muttered, examining his twisted fingers and watching them slowly snap back into place. "This *is* the Tribunal. We landed in it."

CHAPTER 23

"**H**ow could this be the Tribunal?" Max stared into the muddy, dimly lit field surrounding them.

"What part of 'we landed in it' don't you understand? Trust me. I used to have box seats right over there." Humphries pointed at a spot in the bleachers with an air of complete certainty.

"Indeed, you have a great memory," boomed a voice behind them. "Perhaps that's what made you a great Master Boggart. Too bad you chose to throw it all away."

"Mephisto!" gasped Humphries. Max, Derek, and Sam swung around, but none of them could locate the mystery speaker.

"I see you've gained some new friends since we last met. It's a pity to see how prison life has corrupted your character."

"Hey, fathead! Come out here where we can get a good look at you— you coward!" Derek picked up a loose stone and whipped it in the direction of the voice. The rock immediately shot back full force, knocking Derek squarely in the forehead. He fell instantly to the ground, bleeding.

"Enough, Mephisto!" Humphries shouted angrily. "You have nothing better to do these days than pick on helpless fleshies?"

A face the size of a hot air balloon, with eyes the color of burning embers, appeared as if from nowhere and floated in front of Humphries. "Could these fleshies just happen to be the ones that Abaddon is searching for? The ones who possess the manuscript? The ones who have now managed to find a way to our side?" The glowing eyes brightened with intensity with each new question.

"Yes, Mephisto! So they got in! Bingo! But just take a look for yourself. They're harmless. I say we just send them back packing and get on with The Transformation. They will only bring more trouble if they go missing much longer."

"You know the rules, Master Humphries. Their fate is up to the Tribunal, and what do you know?" Mephisto paused, as if for emphasis. "It's now in session!"

The large fiery-eyed face was now joined by an entourage of other ghostly and ghastly faces, each contorting in their expression as they stared down at the four of them.

"Who in the heck are these bozos?" Derek said in a hushed whisper.

"The Tribunal council, Mephisto is Abaddon's main henchman, he does most of the dirty work down here. The others are a bunch of Abaddon suck-ups if there ever were any," Humphries whispered back. "Each one represents a faction here… one for the Wereboars, one for the Changelings, and on and on. All they do is rubber stamp guilty verdicts, but they get extra prana."

A total of seven bobbing heads now floated in front of them, like some weird Halloween holograms, or paper mache heads in a Mardi Gras parade—Max wasn't sure which. There were three on each side of Mephisto, making for a total of seven votes, as if a tie were ever needed. As the Council appeared, shouts of excitement grew as the crowd was admitted to their seats.

"Wow! Word spreads fast," Derek said, eyeing the wild-eyed creatures now filling the seats around them.

"We will start with a reading of the charges," came the thundering voice.

The walking stick Magistrate appeared out of nowhere to reread the charges.

"Violation of Nemesis airspace. Breaching the Outer Threshold."

"Yeah, yeah… disturbing the peace," Derek muttered.

"And disturbing the peace!"

"Do we have a verdict?" bellowed Mephisto. The floating heads rose to each side of Mephisto, drawing together as if to touch heads. Words were briefly exchanged before they returned back to their original slots.

"Yes! We have a verdict," one to the immediate right of Mephisto reported.

"Wait!" This time it was Max. He pushed Humphries to the side and stepped directly in front of the massive head. "You can't do this! You have no authority!"

"No authority?" The face suddenly grew larger, swelling to twice its normal size. "How dare a filthy fleshie address the Tribunal! It's you who has no authority. Guards!"

Max felt stunned at his own burst of boldness, but there was no going back now. He had come too far, endured too much, risked too much, to simply be tossed into some endless Abyss. He had to try something, anything to keep his chance of finding answers about the Vault, but just as importantly, about his father.

A battalion of Barghests approached him, Sam, and Humphries, while another rested his stumpy, hooved foot firmly on the chest of a barely conscious Derek still reeling from the rock to the head.

Humphries leaned forward and whispered hoarsely in Max's ear, "Don't be a fool! You don't know what you're doing."

Emboldened, Max whispered back, "I can handle this, Humphries. I trusted you. Now it's your turn to trust me." Then quickly, turning his head to the side, he whispered back to Sam, "If there was ever a time your love of books could come in handy, it would be now. Where is that passage about the Rule of Judgment?"

Sam's eyes lit up, "Yes, yes, I know exactly what you're talking about, in the back, near the end," she said, flipping furiously until she found it, then shoved the text wide open into Max's hand waiting hands.

Turning to Mephisto, Max announced, "In accordance with the Articles of Nemesis, the Tribunal, consisting of the seven members of the Council of Incubus, can only render a verdict on the inhabitants of Nemesis. As foreigners to this realm, only Abaddon himself can pass judgment."

"Let the Law Be Acknowledged!" came the automatic response from the Council; they could not do otherwise.

Closing the manuscript, Max stared without so much as blinking into the fiery eyes of Mephisto, his face enraged, "I may not have the authority, balloon-brains, but neither do you!"

Derek still wasn't sure what had hit him, a rock, a bird, a plane, but from what he just heard, and from seeing the stars circling around him, he wondered if he was tripping out on some bootlegged prana. Humphries stood likewise in utter amazement. The raucous crowd, hoping to witness an Abyss Toss, grew silent. The massive head grew even larger, inflamed with anger as it drew within inches of Max's face, staring him eye to eye. Max held his ground, his jaw jutting out at the giant head defiantly.

"Everything is not as it appears," he repeated to himself firmly, recalling the words of Zadkiel. As if to prove it, the face grew even redder in appearance, yet Max could feel no heat.

"Very well, then," Mephisto finally pronounced, as if the matter was of no consequence to him. "The Council will defer judgment to Abaddon on the issue." Sam gave a quick fist pump behind Max, bumping him lightly in the back in celebration. The celebration though was premature.

"There is someone, however, who is an inhabitant over whom we *do* have authority."

The eyes of six council members and all the spectators in the stands slowly turned towards Humphries.

"Wait!! No!" Max shouted. "You can't! He's with us! He's our guide, our chaperone! We even made him an honorary fleshie, so you can't do it!" It was utter nonsense, but Max was desperate. It didn't matter anyway because no one paid the slightest attention to his pleas. Six Barghests already had Humphries secured by each of his arms and legs. His eyes said it all.

"Good luck, Max," he murmured. "I tried to warn you, but there's never going to be a way to win this."

Reinvigorated, the crowd now chanted wildly, throwing small rodent-like creatures into the arena. The frantic critters scrambled about as the onlookers danced in what can only be described as a form of mass hysteria. Max looked down at Derek who was still holding onto his head.

"Derek, are you alright? He really beaned you, didn't he?"

"Yeah… man, that guy should pitch for the Red Sox," he groaned as he got to his feet. There was already a golf ball-sized lump on his forehead, but the bleeding had stopped. "What's going on, Max? Hey, where's Humprhies?"

"They've called for Abaddon and they're taking Humphries to the Abyss. I've got to come up with a plan."

"Wow!" he said, casting a look over at Sam. "I'm out for all of ten minutes and things somehow go from bad to worse."

"Look, Derek, I get that things have not gone according to plan, but I could really use some help here."

Just then a huge rumbling sound echoed throughout the Assembly arena. The ground underneath Max and Derek began to shake violently. Then a deafening *crack!* filled the air as the arena floor began to split apart.

"No way! What is it about earthquakes and fault lines around here?"

"This is no earthquake, Derek! It's the Abyss. Quick, jump to this side!"

Derek leapt over the widening crack, still surrounded by a host of Barghests. The divide widened until it was apparent the center of the arena sat upon a huge, mechanized plate that opened like a giant eyelid, revealing nothing but infinite blackness below. Max felt an icy blast of air shoot up, knocking him and Derek off their feet. The Barghests holding Humphries dragged him to the edge of the yawning black hole.

The once roaring crowd quickly fell silent in anticipation as all eyes turned to the floating head of Mephisto, a grossly twisted smile spreading across his face. Slowly, deliberately, he nodded his approval. The masses yelled triumphantly. Humphries let out a scream as the six Barghests swung him back and then hurled him into the pitch-black void below.

For a moment, all stood still, trapped in time. Humphries' sprawling body spun in a slow-motion spiral, turning over once, twice, and then a third time, before plummeting into the black vortex. Max also screamed but couldn't hear his own voice over the roar of the cheering crowd. He watched every second of the scene as it replayed over and over in his mind, as if it were a visual form of déjà vu, one that repeated like a cruel, endless loop. The image of Humphries falling so helplessly, eyes wide with fear, burnt like hot embers into Max's mind.

Gone.

Just like my dad.

No notice, no warning, no heads up. Just the black emptiness of an inexplicable darkness staring back.

"Max! Run!" It was Sam. Several Barghests had grabbed both her and Derek, but it was too late, they now had their vice grips on him as well.

"Well, well, it seems like things are wrapping up nicely," came the now familiar raspy voice of Mephisto. "And since you insisted on keeping us all waiting in suspense, it would only be rude if I did not return the favor!"

Max could only imagine what awaited him next. Rotting in prison? Being fed to a horde of hungry Hobgoblins? But nothing. Then, a few scattered shadows appeared on the Assembly floor in front of him, as if something above blocked what little light that shone. He glanced up to see not so itsy-bitsy spiders, the size of large watermelons with thick hairy legs, quickly rappelling down their long silky lengths of rope toward them.

"That's right, Max," Mephisto laughed. "Since you wanted to 'hang around' a little longer, I thought I would oblige!"

WHACK!

WHACK! WHACK!

Max felt something smack his right ankle, then his left. Suddenly he found himself flipped upside down, his feet now pointing upwards, wrapped tightly together, hanging quite literally by a thread. The large spider-like creatures had spun an additional string or two of the gooey thread around his feet, and then hoisted him and the others in the air, suspended from the Assembly rafters. They now hung just a foot or two off the Assembly floor, inches from the edge of The Abyss.

"It's no use. There's no escaping this time," Mephisto laughed thunderously. "Your personal travel guide and 'honorary fleshie' has gone on permanent vacation and *you* have an appointment with Abaddon. So, I suggest you rest up! And if you should perchance wiggle your way out of this one, then have a nice fall!" This time, Mephisto was joined in his laughter by the roaring faces of the six other Council members.

With that, the flaming head of Mephisto disappeared, along with the six Council members, evaporating back into the darkness from which they appeared. The thronging crowd of onlookers was also gone, their appetite for horror now momentarily appeased. The arena grew dark and silent, all sense of hope fading with it. Every time he closed his eyes, Max could only see Humphries' frightened face. The time for thinking and fast action was over. In the emptiness of the chamber, all Max could sense was his failure.

"Max…"

"What?" Max replied.

Derek was now hanging upside down alongside him. "I just want to say—"

"Yeah, I know, Derek, all my plans go from bad to worse; I agree, it's all my fault. Here we all are, hanging upside down over the very Abyss I was supposed to avoid."

"No, I was going to say I know how you felt about Humphries…" Derek stammered. "And even though things are looking bad right now, I'm sorry I said all that stuff about him. I mean, he turned out to be okay, and I guess I should've trusted you about him—that's all."

Max tried to move his feet, which were already hurting from the tight webbing. He felt limp and exhausted, his body along with the other two, gently swaying back and forth over the lip of The Abyss.

"No, Derek, it's the other way around. I'm the one who should have trusted you. You said not to come here. You told me not to get Humphries involved. Not to do any of this! But I just kept pushing it, thinking I could solve everything. And all I've done is to make a mess of everything—for all of us, you, Sam and especially for Humphries."

"It's not… like… we… didn't… volunteer," Sam added in, twisting around to see if she could reach up to her feet somehow to untether herself. But it was no use, the silky strands were thick and strong, like parachute rope.

Max looked down and let his hands fall to the ground, touching it as he swayed back and forth. "Professor von Guttenberg, Zadkiel—they both trusted me. Here I thought that maybe, just maybe, I could do something to save the situation. Forget friends, I couldn't even save a supposed enemy!"

"Well, you've saved me, Max. More than once, I might add," Derek insisted reassuringly. "And hey, this isn't over yet, right? Maybe Abaddon turns out to be a myth, or he's for real but gets called away on some important business. It can still work out, Max! It has so far—sort of." Derek twisted around for a moment, fighting his bindings. "Maybe we can climb these rope things to the top of here and… Max? Max? What do you think?"

But Max had somehow, out of sheer exhaustion, fallen asleep. Visions of narks, hobgoblins, and wereboars danced in his head, swooping and clawing and baring their bloody, sharp teeth. He saw himself running through the endless tunnels that had led him to this place. Every turn he took brought more danger until, at last, he saw a light ahead. He raced breathlessly toward the light and once there, found an open door that he immediately slammed shut. *Safe at last!* he thought. The darkness was gone and in its place was…

The back room of his uncle's bookstore…?

"Things turned out a little bit different than you expected, have they?" came the familiar voice.

"Zadkiel!" Max looked up to see the bearded giant floating near the top row of a bookshelf, thumbing through an out-of-print, old World Atlas as he spoke.

"Different! Yes, I would say so! Nothing has turned out right. I have no idea how to stop this Abaddon, how to find the Vault, or any clue whatsoever about my father, everything's a mystery within a mystery, and now it looks like it was all for nothing. I need your help, Zadkiel. You are from Empyrean, you must have some tricks, some powers, some answers, you must know something, anything!"

"I only know that you know, Max. And of that I am certain."

"But how can that be? I'm failing!"

"Really? As I recall, you stared Mephisto in the face and quoted to him from his own law. You've managed to keep the faith and confidence of your best friends, and you fought to save a former enemy, the Boggart. You have not done so badly, Max. As I said before, all is not as it appears. There is more to you, Max, than what you know—find out what that is."

"Then what do I do next?"

"The thing you must do."

"Uh… face Abaddon!"

"The final enemy must be confronted!" Zadkiel agreed. "And only you can do that, Max."

"Only me? Why out of this entire planet did it come down to me, Max Kellerman of Providence, Rhode Island? Explain that to me, would you?"

"Because, Max, only you are you. A key opens one lock, but not another. Your choice is to do or to not do."

"But what if I *can't* do?"

"More importantly, what if you can?"

The light around Zadkiel brightened to the point that he could no longer make out his form. Max held his hands up to shield his eyes from the blinding glare, and he was gone.

CHAPTER 24

Max's eyes snapped open wide. "Derek, where's the Extractor gun you had?"

"Huh? The Extractor?"

"The Time Extractor! The one I had you grab just before we got blown out of the prison. Where did it go?"

"Look," Sam yelled, "over there, it must have gotten knocked loose from Derek's hands and landed by the stairs, the ones leading up to the Assembly seating."

"What do you think, Sam? Can we swing ourselves that far over there?"

"Not sure, that's quite a ways," Sam said, "and besides, as we swing, the rope would rise higher off the ground, so I don't think so."

"What about the Boggart's survival belt—anything useful there?" Max said, eyeing the belt around Derek's waist.

"We've been through this already, Max. There's not much there; it's basically Boggart personal care."

"Look again!"

"All right, all right, Jeez. Let's see…" Derek again felt around his mud-caked waist and shook his head. "Nope, there's just that glowing prison key, the holder where the detonator went and some little bottles and gadgets that look like Boggart mouthwash, a bottle of slime coat, nail clippers…"

"But Zadkiel said…"

"Wait! You *spoke* to Zadkiel?! He's here? Where? Can he get us out of here?"

"No, nothing like that. It was one of those… well… never mind. Anyway, he said I'd know what to do, but I'm still not sure! Everything keeps coming to a dead end."

Derek grimaced at the expression. He wasn't used to seeing Max without answers. It was simply Max's nature to solve things. But for now, he seemed stumped.

"What do you think Abaddon's going to do to us, Max?" Sam said, exhausted from reaching up and trying to loosen the sticky strands from around her feet.

"Most likely the same thing Mephisto did to Humphries. Unless…"

"Unless what? Unless what, Max?"

Max said nothing for a moment as the internal wheels turned. Then his face lit up with a renewed sense of urgency. "Derek, Sam, we've gotta get out of here!"

"No duh! Of course, we've gotta get out of here. Otherwise, we're vapor dust."

"No! It's more than just us. If we can get out, I think there's a way to stop the time machine *and* save Humphries."

"Uh, Max? Humphries is gone, poof! Have you lost it, buddy? Take a look around you. We're upside down here swinging over a real-life black hole, and our one guy on the inside was shrink-wrapped into a speck of nothingness."

"No, not nothingness, Derek. Only complete *nothingness* is nothingness. Humphries said that all time gets removed until only the thought of you is left. Remember? There's still something there… the thought itself."

"That's all that's ever left of a person, Max… the thoughts, the memories," Sam said, wiggling herself around to face Max. "I'm not following."

"So, what if the thought of the person is what remains and holds space for them? Like a dry sponge. Maybe time is like water, and Humphries was simply freeze-dried."

Derek paused for a moment as the possibility began to sink in.

"Are you saying we'd just need to add time back in and he'd reappear?"

"It's a possibility, isn't it? Any crazier than how we got here in the first place? One hundred twenty-six sneezes—remember, Derek?"

"And you're suggesting we get all this time from…"

"The Time Extractor! I'll explain later. You said something about Boggart nail clippers, can you reach them?"

"Yeah, I think so, they're here somewhere, around the backside," Derek felt around his waist, searching, "Oh, I think these are it!"

"Great!" Max exclaimed with growing excitement. "See if you can reach up and use them to cut yourself loose."

"But we're awfully close to the lip of The Abyss," Sam said, eyeing the yawning chasm. "He could fall right in."

"Not if he times it right!" Max insisted. "Derek, start swinging back and forth, then start cutting the line. Once it's almost through, cut the final thread when you're safely away from the edge."

"Easy for you to say, I have no sense of rhythm," he complained.

"Just do it, it should work!"

"Should," Derek said again mumbling, and he pulled open the razor-sharp Boggart clippers, bending himself back and forth to build up momentum.

"Okay, that's good enough, you're swinging far enough away to land safely; now just cut it!"

Derek had already cut several of the strands of silky rope, with just one remaining.

"I don't know, Max…"

"Just cut it, Derek!"

SNAP!

Before Derek could bend up to cut the remaining final cord, it suddenly broke. Derek fell instantly, crashing into the very outside lip of the Abyss just as it was swinging back to clear it. He felt the blow to his ribs as he desperately tried to gain a grip on the hard metallic Assembly floor, the Boggart clippers bouncing loose as he did so.

"Hold on, Derek!" Sam screamed.

"Sam, push me!" Max yelled. "I might be able to reach him."

"I'm falling!" Derek screeched, with only one hand now holding on.

With all her might, Sam pushed hard against Max, sending him swinging toward Derek. With his one available hand, Derek reached for Max, grabbing just enough of one hand to hang on.

"Hold tight!" Max yelled, as they now swung back over the very center of The Abyss. "Don't look down Derek!" Max cautioned, a blast of endless, cold air streaming up, howling in their ears, as they held tight to each other's hands. The rope finally swung back, and with a mighty thrust, Max let go of Derek, sending him tumbling to the Assembly floor.

"Quick!" Max yelled, swinging back out over The Abyss. "Find the clippers, get Sam down."

Derek scrambled frantically on hands and knees, finally locating the clippers a few feet away. Standing up, he grabbed hold of Sam, still hanging head down, right at the lip of the dark chasm.

"Hold still," Derek instructed, "I think I can reach up and cut this," he said, making sure that when he did, she was safely away from the edge.

Crash!

Sam fell hard to the ground and stayed there, feeling the firm surface like it was a friend.

"What about Max, Derek!" she said looking back into the empty blackness. Suddenly, Max swung back into sight.

"Got him!" Derek said, grabbing hold again, this time not letting go. Derek made quick work of the silky rope, cutting Max loose while holding him tight around the waist. They collapsed together on the Assembly floor in a mashed-up pile of arms and legs. *Safe at last,* Max thought for all of five seconds, but he was wrong.

CHAPTER 25

Zzaammm!

Max heard Sam let out a piercing scream. As he turned, he saw what appeared to be a dozen or more Boggarts charging the cage, each with a Time Extractor in hand aimed in their direction. Unfortunately, Sam had taken the first shot.

"Max… do something!" Derek pleaded. A second blast whizzed by and nearly hit Max.

These Time Extractors seem to be the weapon of choice down here, he thought. "Ahhhh!"

Derek took a glancing shot to the arm. "They're sucking the living daylights out of us, Max!"

"Quick, Derek, grab that Time Extractor, the one by the stairs!"

Wanna play that way, he thought, *we'll fight fire with fire.*

"Toss it here!" he yelled, and with one quick flip, The Extractor was airborne. Max reached up, clutching the familiar object in his hands, then spun back around.

Zzaaaammmm! the blast sounded as this time Max opened fire back at the frenzied mass of Boggarts. The biggest one fell back dazed but more pressed in. *Zzaaaammm!* Max fired again repeatedly, but it served only to slow the return fire. *Zzaaaammm!* This time Max was hit. His head reeled from the shock.

They must have set the guns to the highest suction time possible, Max thought, triggering off another volley of shots. *I feel like I'm losing days, not seconds.*

"There's too many of them, Max… think of something else. Quick!" Derek was now on the floor huddled up in a ball.

"Hang on, Derek!" Max maneuvered to protect Derek and fired repeatedly into the mob until the gun fell silent.

"What's the matter!" Derek shouted.

"It's overheated. It won't fire!"

"HOLD ON!" came the angry shout. It was Sam.

Having no weapon, she had run full blast back toward the ropes hanging by the Abyss. Grabbing hold, she swung out in a huge arc over the void, and then returning, both feet out, knocked down an entire row of Boggarts.

"Nice work, Sam!" Max yelled, letting out a whoop.

Max now held the gun itself up into the air to deflect the life sucking neon rays coming at them. Pulling up close to Derek, he frantically searched the Boggart survival belt again, throwing anything he found at the attackers, all in hopes that one of the items would prove helpful. Sam joined in.

"There's nothing left," she said, "what now?"

With every object gone from the belt, Max charged at the approaching wall of Boggarts. Three shots hit him dead-center in his chest flying him backwards, landing again beside Sam and Derek, before rolling over on his side.

"Hey," Derek gasped, "you okay?"

"Yeah… hold on… I'll think of something." But at this point Max's voice was more of a whisper. He felt all energy draining from his exhausted body. Memories of his parents, school, and his long afternoons at the bookstore, all flashed in front of him and went up in smoke. His chest ached where he had been shot, and so did most other parts of his body. He reached up to touch his chest, seeing if the shots had left any visible marks, and felt a familiar egg-shaped object…

"Zadkiels' stone! What…"

Max was still wearing the orb around his neck. He felt it warming in his hand.

Part of a bigger story, he recalled Zadkiel's words. *Well, if it's part of the story, it has to be now, or there won't be a story.*

Mustering all remaining energy, Max jumped back up to his feet, clutching the stone in his right hand.

"Whatever you got, throw it at them, Max!" Derek shouted.

"Yeah Max, do it!"

Max cocked his right hand back, wincing from the pain. Clenching his teeth, he took aim at the advancing Boggarts when all at once a blinding iridescent green light shot from the center of the stone, splitting in every direction.

"The Eye!" the Boggarts screamed, falling back at once, tripping over each other's flailing arms and legs. Max stood dumbstruck as scores of panic-stricken Boggarts galloped off in ape-like fashion, littering the ground with their abandoned Time Extractors. Max again felt the pulsating warmth of the stone. The outside of it was now crystal clear except for what appeared to be the emerald-green circle, the marble sized gem in its center. As Max drew the stone closer to examine it, the light receded.

"Wow. What was *that* all about?" Derek shifted his weight to sit up, still holding the side where he had taken most of the shots.

"I'm not sure," Max replied in a quiet voice. "Apparently, Zadkiel's stone has some kick to it."

"Well, whatever you do, hold onto it!" Derek insisted.

Max gently put the stone back around his neck. Then he turned his attention to Derek. "How are you feeling? You don't look so good."

"Yeah. Kind of like that day when I had the snot beat out of me in double elimination dodgeball—only fifty million times worse."

"How about you, Sam, are you okay?"

"Yeah," she replied, brushing it off, "I think they got their paybacks."

"Well, let's get moving. There's no telling when they'll be back with more."

"But we still have no way of getting out of here, Max! The Time Extractors are only good for sucking life."

"Yeah, sucking out life and restoring it."

CHAPTER 26

"**D**erek, Sam, quick—gather up these extra Time Extractors the Boggarts dropped and head back to the Abyss!"

"Back to the Abyss?" Derek questioned, as he and Sam gathered up several of the abandoned Extractors, slinging them over their shoulders and running to catch Max, who was grabbing several of his own along the way.

"What about their survival belts?!" Derek shouted after him.

"Yeah, grab a couple extras of those, too." Max was now back at the edge of the bottomless Abyss. He could feel the eerie, cold blast of air blowing upward and chilling his bones. Derek arrived alongside, still puffing hard from the run and the weight of four Extractors wrapped about his body, two on each side. The mouth of the Abyss revealed a darkness deeper than any starless night. Its pitch-black color seemed to absorb what little light there was.

Max reached around his neck and removed Zadkiel's stone once again. He clutched it tightly in his palm, feeling it slowly begin to warm.

"What are you doing, Max?"

"The only thing I know to do. There's no way I can see down there, but there is something that can—an Eye, like this one."

He unclenched his hand and held the stone over the Abyss. Bright beams of light shot out, penetrating the dark interior of the bottomless pit.

"I don't see anything," Sam said. "Do you?"

"No, but let's double-check the edges. Maybe he got lucky and fell on a ledge."

Max strained to see any sign of movement, but all was still and silent.

"Look!" Derek pointed just above the center of the opening. "It looks like a tiny dust speck in the light."

Max squinted and looked harder. In the middle of the one of the rays of light was the smallest of particles, like the type one often sees floating in a ray of morning light. The very type that often made him sneeze.

"That must be it, Derek!"

"But how do you know that little speck is Humphries?"

"He was the last one thrown in, so I figure he must be near the top, just waiting to float down over time." It was just an assumption, but it sounded logical. "Hit it, Derek!"

Derek switched on an Extractor, pressed the orange button, and aimed at the nearest speck. *Zzzaaammm!* The jagged bolt missed the tiny speck and shot off into the darkness below. Instantly, a wereboar roared out of the Abyss and came lunging toward him.

"Reverse it!" Max yelled. "Reverse it!" Just as quickly as he fired, Derek flipped the switch and sucked the horned mutant back down to a particle.

Derek gave a low whistle. "Wow, that was close! You wanna give it a try?"

Max nodded and took the Extractor. "C'mon, Humphries… you must be here. I *need* you to be here." Max aimed at the miniscule dried-up speck, held his breath, and then slowly pulled the trigger.

Zzzaaammm!

A whirling ball of arms and legs instantly appeared and came crashing down on him, knocking him off his feet and rolling back within inches of the Abyss itself.

"Humphries?"

The twisting bunch of arms and legs flipped and flopped about before finally coming to a halt. Max stepped closer and blinked at the familiar face of his lost friend.

"Humphries! You're back!" Max fell on top of Humphries, squeezing him hard around his thick waist. Derek came bounding over along with Sam as they both piled on top of Max and Humphries, knocking them all down.

"Nice work!!" Derek shouted to Max as Humphries lay dazed and disoriented on the ground.

"Humphries, do you know where you are?" Max asked, now straddling the fat figure, giving him a gentle back and forth slap to each of his sagging cheeks, as if to help him wake up.

PJ DAVIS

"No… I only remember falling… and blankness… and Mephisto!! Why, that good for nothing match head… wait till I…"

"Never mind!" Max exclaimed. "We just need to get moving before every Nark, Boggart, Barghest, and Wereboar this side of The Threshold comes here to finish us off for good. Humphries, what's the best way outta here?"

Humphries pointed all six hands toward a cluster of buildings several off in the distance. "You can see the top of The Vault from here, just over that top row of the Assembly seating."

"The Vault?" Max paused, thinking for a moment.

"What? What's the matter, Max?" Sam asked.

"Yeah," Derek chimed in. "There it is, The Vault, so what are we waiting for?"

"There's one more stop we—*I*—need to make," Max said.

"Where's that?" Sam asked.

"Quandary."

"Max, I told you, that's a bad idea!" Humphries insisted. "You don't know what you're getting yourself into."

"You said yourself that's where they keep prisoners. My dad could be there."

"Could, Max, but unlikely," Humphries continued. "But more than that, no one comes back the same from Quandary, if they come back at all. Let's get on with the Vault, there isn't much time."

"NO!" Max insisted. "You guys can go on, but I have to do this."

"Where is this place," Sam asked. "Is it close by?"

"Unfortunately, yes," Humphries sighed. "Right outside the Assembly, between here and The Vault, what a happy coincidence," he continued, shrugging his shoulders.

"Then let's go!" Max said, his energy renewed.

"Not that way! You'll be seen immediately. There's an underground passage reserved strictly for Boggarts. It leads directly to the Vault. There's an entrance to Quandary on the way."

Derek perked up. "What? Another Boggart expressway?"

Humphries nodded and motioned to the back of the Assembly. "That wall there… there's an opening that goes down one level."

Max moved forward and then stopped abruptly. "Humphries…"

148

"Yes, Max?"

"You've done more than I could have ever asked. It's up to us now. I want you to know that as far as I'm concerned, you're free to go." Max tossed a spare Time Extractor in Humphries' direction. Startled, the Boggart grasped hold of the device, gripping it, and then turning it over in his webbed hands, as if reacquainting himself with an old friend. He raised the Extractor to one eye for good measure, staring down the barrel and pulling the trigger on an imaginary target. Flipping it straight up again, Humphries gave the weapon a big wet kiss.

"You think I'm going to stop now? After what they did to me? Seven hundred sixty-seven years of faithful service and for what? Max, do you think anyone else would have come back for me? Heck, *I* wouldn't have come back for me. No, this is now my battle, too, for better or worse. Let's get this over with."

As he led the way into the passage, Max, Derek, and Sam exchanged a quick grin and fell in close behind the emboldened Boggart. Max felt a renewed confidence now that they were once again a foursome. It felt more like a small army, an invincible one. But as they entered the lower level of the arena, that feeling quickly vaporized into a whole new terror.

CHAPTER 27

"There must be thousands of these things!" Derek half-shouted, half-whispered in his excitement.

"These 'things' are Boggarts," Humphries corrected him, appalled at Derek's insensitivity. "And you're going to have to keep the comments down—we don't want to set the alarm off."

"They have an alarm system here?" Derek asked, amazed at the thought.

"What, you think you have all the technology?"

Max rolled his eyes. "Guys, am I going to have to call a time-out!" He turned to Humphries and sighed. "Okay, what's the plan?"

"My plan? I don't have a plan."

"Then why did you have us come down here?"

"So we wouldn't get caught up there!" he said, pointing his fingers excitedly. "You want a plan? Here's mine—it's called 'hiding.'"

"Or you show them the Eye!" Sam suggested.

"What 'eye'?" asked Humphries.

Max squirmed uncomfortably for a moment. "It's nothing, just something someone gave me once." He shot a warning glance back in Sam's direction.

Startled, Humphries stepped back a few feet. "Tell me you don't have *the* Eye…"

Max bit his lip and nodded slowly, realizing that anything Zadkiel gave him would most likely be bad news to a Boggart. "I had no idea what it was… Zadkiel gave it to me, and it had this writing on it… here, look."

"No! Don't touch it! I'll be toast in two seconds!" Humphries' three eyes widened in horror. "Max, what on Abaddon's grave are you doing with that thing!"

"Zadkiel said it was a reminder, a way to keep in touch."

"Well, I for one don't need any reminding, thank you."

"What do you know about this thing, Humphries?" Sam asked.

"Know about it?! It's the Eye! As in THE EYE! It sees everything and it sees nothing."

"Yeah, that makes total sense," Derek muttered.

"The Eye sees only truth, nothing else. So if it flashes on anything untrue or unreal, it vanishes. *Zap!* Just like that."

"What do you mean? 'The truth'? Everything we see is the truth," Derek insisted.

Humphries sighed with exasperation. "Not exactly. Everything you see down here, and much of what you see in your world, is based on fear. Fear is nothing—it's an illusion. You see it because you believe in it, and because you believe in it… it becomes 'real.' It's hard to explain."

"So then, you're not real?" asked Max.

Humphries looked down at his feet. "No. Not in the big scheme of things. Down here I'm real and most of the time in your world. But those who can really see… well, they see that I'm nothing."

The four of them sat in silence for a long moment. Humphries continued his downward stare. "I guess I'm not really much help at this point," he said quietly. "Maybe I should just get going. You've got the Eye, so you're all set."

"Wait!" Max grabbed Humphries' arm as he started to pull away. "You say the Eye can only see the truth, but it saw you!"

Humphries stopped and turned around. For the first time he was speechless.

"It's true!" Sam said. "The eye showed us where you were in the Abyss."

Humphries shook his head. "But how could that be? It can't be! I'm nothing, a thief among thieves. Are you sure it was the Eye that saw me and not an Extractor beam?"

"Sure as I am that you're a Master Boggart that can get us out of here," Max insisted.

Humphries let the words roll around in his head for a moment, then nodded to himself. Pointing down the tunnel to his left, he said, "We're about a nark drag away from the Time Vault itself; Quandary is just up ahead."

"A 'nark drag'?"

"It's the distance a Nark can drag a Wereboar before letting go. About a quarter mile, or four hundred of your Earth meters."

"Actually, we don't use metric much, not like in Europe, although our sodas are two liters—"

"Quiet!" Max whispered. "What's that?"

The constant humming sound from the Vault, the one that reverberated throughout Nemesis, had suddenly stopped. They had become so accustomed to the constant droning that the silence seemed deafening in comparison.

"That's not a good sign," Humphries said. "The Time Vault is always in operation. They would only shut it down if it was at full capacity."

A long, low horn sounded, a forlorn sound, like those made from a giant conch shell echoing out over an ocean. Then silence. The army of Boggarts, Time Extractors still in hand, suddenly turned about-face and marched directly at them, heading down the passage towards the Assembly.

"It's time!!" Humphries gasped.

"Time for what?" Sam asked.

"Time for the Transformation. And it can only be declared by Abaddon himself."

"No! Not yet—" Derek objected.

"Yes," Humphries said, and gulped hard. "He's going to start the invasion as soon as they can distribute the contents of the Vault. That's why they're heading to the Assembly; it's designed for the Transformation, which is the only place big enough to house everyone. Pipes from the Time Vault go right into the Assembly seating area. They can just turn open the valve on the Vault and the prana will flow right in there, right into feeding troughs in the stands, so they can just lap it all up."

"Look out! Here they come!" shouted Sam.

Max, Sam, and Derek crept back and ducked behind a small outcropping of rock, smashing themselves tight behind Humphries. Soon, the thundering six-legged footsteps of hundreds of Boggarts, armed with Time Extractors, came stampeding by. Max, Sam, and Derek could make out the shadows of their oversized heads parading against the tunnel wall.

When the final Boggart passed, Max asked, "How much time do we have, Humphries?"

"Not much. Abaddon will address the entire Assembly while a few remaining Vault workers prepare the disbursement tubes that flow into the Assembly area. Once he's done, the tubes will be opened, the prana will flow, and the feeding will begin. That's when things will really get interesting."

"Interesting as in everything here will begin to transform?"

Humphries nodded solemnly.

"Then what?" asked Derek.

"Then you'll be history."

Max had heard enough. He was already off running down the eerily silent tunnel, his footsteps echoing behind. "C'mon, Humphries, he's heading to that Quandary place, and we can't let him go in there alone!" Derek shouted. The three of them followed after Max in close pursuit.

"So, this is it?" Max said, standing in front of a single door, cut out from the stone passageway, a sign above reading, QUANDARY, ENTER AT YOUR OWN RISK.

"Yep, that's it, Max."

"But there's no one here, no guards, no gate, no nothing."

"Quandary doesn't need a guard, it's its own guard."

"Another 'system'?" asked Sam.

"Sort of—not sure since I've never met anyone who's come back," Humphries replied, shaking his head.

Max reached for the latch to enter.

"Wait! Max! Are you sure you want to do this?" asked Sam, looking him in the eyes.

"I have to, Sam. I can't go back without answers; I have to know why," he said. Turning back, he glanced at Humphries and then Derek. "I'm sorry, I know we had a plan, but I need to do this one extra thing. I will be back, I promise."

And with that, he was gone.

CHAPTER 28

White. White everywhere. Above, below, all around him. "Wait? Where is this? I thought Nemesis was all darkness."

"Can I help you?" came a small voice from somewhere ahead.

"Help me? Who's asking?"

"I am, of course," came the voice of the receptionist. Max looked ahead to see what appeared to be a small circular desk, as white as everything else around him, with an insect-like creature seated in a chair behind it. The closest way Max could describe it would be a cricket, half the size of a human, with eyes on the ends of its antenna, busily scanning some documents in front of it.

"Did you have an appointment?"

"Uh, no, not exactly," Max hesitated.

"Oh! Alright, you could have called ahead, busy week, what's the name you're looking for?" the smallish cricket-like creature asked, peering closer. "Say, you don't look like you're from around here?"

"No, just visiting actually," Max demurred. "The person, I mean, the name I'm looking for is Kellerman, Nathaniel Kellerman. He would have been brought here sometime…"

"Oh yes! He's here alright! Caught in transition, very unfortunate case. Seems he was trying to enter and never quite made it through. Really scrambled him up, not much left really, and that was *before* the interrogations."

"He's here, then! Can you show me?"

"I can show you what's left of him, but that's all you get, and we close soon, so you'll have to make it quick." With that, the pokey-eyed creature pushed a couple of buttons under the desk, and a smooth, grayish white, slightly marble-colored tablet, rose up from the middle of the desk, resting just inches in front of Max's face.

"Here, let me help dial this up," she said, walking around the desk to help. She pushed a few more buttons, and the tablet began to vibrate, then jitter, and then finally, an image appeared. It looked to be a fuzzy face, eyes closed, coming in and out of focus until, at last, it locked into place.

"Dad!" Max shouted. "Dad, it's me, Max!!"

"I think I should let you two have time to yourselves," the insect receptionist said, scurrying off with some paperwork. "I'll be back soon to close."

Max looked again at the screen. He could see the pupils under the eyelids stirring around, as if processing information, and then, gradually they opened.

"Max? Max, is that you?"

"Dad! You're here! You're alive!"

"Max, are you there, son? Max, I miss you… I miss you so much."

"Yes, yes, I'm here. Dad, where do they have you? I can come get you!"

"I—I'm not sure Max. I haven't been feeling like myself." The eyes searched around and then met Max's. "I was so busy, so busy with work, and then there was this thing, this dark energy, it was absorbing everything! I knew I had to find it, stop it, but I'm not sure what happened. Where are you, Max?"

"Never mind, I'll explain later. How can I find you? Do you remember what they did with you?"

"They kept asking questions, so many questions." A look of pain came over his father's face.

"Dad, I can't stay long, I need to know where to find you."

"I don't know, Max," his father replied, the image beginning to flicker in and out again. "That night… I knew I was taking a chance…" The image disappeared and came on again. "I just know that I had to make a choice, a difficult one, and now you'll have to do the same."

"But I can't leave you!" Max insisted. "Not after finally finding you. It's not right—it's not fair!" Max's eyes filled with tears.

"I know, Max, but life is not always fair," his father said, his eyes looking directly into Max's, as the image began to slowly fade. "Just remember son, *I'm right here with you, and whatever is out there, you can face it.*"

"Well, unfortunately, it's closing time!" came the voice of the buggy receptionist, giving a quick flip of a button, causing the stone tablet to start descending.

"I love you Max, I always will…" the voice trailed off.

"Wait! Wait a minute!" Max shouted at the hurried insect. "Where is he at, where can I find him?"

"Who knows, maybe in the back in suspension, perhaps stored in a memory stone, who's to say really? Transitions are messy. I know they've been working on his case for some time now. You're welcome to take a look around, but trust me, it will take quite some time. There's no end in sight to all the storage back there."

"Time is the one thing I don't have!" Max insisted.

"Well, it's now or never," the impatient receptionist replied.

"Why is that?" Max asked.

"You weren't told?" she replied. "I thought everyone knew."

"Knew what?"

"You only get one visit here to Quandary—once you leave, you can never return. You can go out this back door and keep searching for whatever it is you think you've lost, or you can leave through the front door, the way you came in, and get on with your business. The choice is entirely yours."

Max felt a sudden rumble.

"Oh my!" the insect said. "Sounds like there's a gathering at the Assembly. So, what will it be?"

The room shook again, then again.

"I'm sorry, Dad," Max said between fitful tears. "The time has come; I have to make a choice, too." With that, he turned and bolted back toward the entrance door. As he opened it to leave, he read the sign above.

Quandary
Once you leave, there's no return.

CHAPTER 29

"Quick, grab the Extractors up, we gotta get to that Vault!" Max yelled, bursting through the door, and heading down the tunnel.

"Wait!" Sam shouted. "What did you find out about—"

"There's no time to talk about it, let's just get moving," Max said.

"Jeez, what's up with that?" Derek wondered aloud.

"I told you," Humphries said, trailing behind them, shaking his head along the way, "they never come out quite right once they go in there."

At the end of the tunnel, Max motioned back to the rest of the group to proceed with caution. Up ahead was something Max had never expected. In place of what he thought would be a massive industrial complex, he saw what can only be described as a farming operation. In place of an iron clad vault, there stood an enormous tree—at least a hundred feet tall. Glowing red objects bobbed around it, adorning each branch. The entire trunk seemed to sway back and forth, not because of wind because there wasn't any, but as if the tree itself was twisting, moving, with branches outstretched as if to show off its glowing fruits. Staring up at it, Max felt at once amazed and slightly queasy. Around its massive base, large pipes were driven into the ground at a 45-degree angle, as if by some design.

"What is this place?" Max asked Humphies. "I thought you said we were heading to the Vault?"

"We are at the Vault, it's right over there," he said pointing to a rising summit in the background, a volcano-shaped formation made of pure granite, a puff of smoke rising from its peak.

"Then what is this?" Sam asked, pointing up at the tree.

"I'll explain, but first we have to get across this last little bitty ridge; it's the one last line of defense to protect the Vault."

"Of course, there's one more," Derek moaned.

The towering tree, and the looming Vault behind it, sat on a large outcropping of rock, an island of stone as it were, with the only access being a razor thin pathway that served as a narrow bridge.

"Only Boggarts have the sense of balance needed to cross this," Humphries bragged, "that plus our six feet. But no worries," he said, scooping up Sam and Derek and placing them on his broad shoulders.

"Max, climb up there, too," he instructed. "I can walk us across."

Derek and Sam reached down, and pulled Max up, in between them.

"Are you sure about this, Humphries?" Max asked, eyeing the drop-off below.

"A walk in the park," Humphries said, taking the first step.

With a careful, measured pace, he stepped delicately across the razor-thin pathway. A few small pebbles scattered into the drop-off. Derek couldn't bear to look down, so he stared straight ahead into the bright lights radiating from the fruit on the tree ahead. What he saw made no sense.

"Wait! Hey! Are those giant apples?!"

"Derek, not now! Believe it or not, this requires a high degree of concentration, even for an experienced Boggart. Just don't move." Humphries had to use all six feet to cross the ridge, two on the spine of the ridge itself and two on each side of it to stabilize his weight.

"But Humphries, just look… there's hundreds of them, and boy, do they look delicious." Derek leaned forward to point, causing Humphries to lose his balance. Derek began to slip off, grabbing hold of Sam, who held on to Max, who held on for dear life.

"Gotcha!" Humphries said, pushing Derek back up.

"Hold tight this time, Derek, and stop thinking about food!" Max shouted.

"Alright already!" Derek said. A nervous drop of sweat beaded on Derek's forehead before falling to the ground.

Crraasssh!!

"What th—"

"The ridge, it's crumbling, Humphries, run!" Max shouted. The drop of human sweat ate like acid through the thin strip of rock.

"The rock senses human presence! I forgot to mention not to sweat." The passageway behind them began to break away and fall in large chunks. Humphries swung his arms around wildly for balance, but it was no use, the ridge completely collapsed.

But then absolutely nothing happened.

Max opened his eyes only to see himself floating in midair. He, Sam, and Derek, all still on Humphries' back, were somehow just hovering. He looked down and saw Humphries beating all six arms furiously.

"Max, Sam, Derek, jump off, quick!"

One by one, the threesome lunged onto the outcropping where the imposing tree sat towering above them. They rolled onto their backs to witness Humphries gracefully float over and ease down to the ground.

"You *fly?*" Derek shouted angrily at Humphries. "You fly, and we're just now finding this out?"

Humphries gasped and held up a weak hand as if to ask for a moment. "Only in extreme emergencies," he said in a gasping breath. "It drains energy out of me like Hobgoblins on a feeding frenzy."

Derek snapped, "Well, I can think of about a dozen previous occasions when that would have qualified!"

"C'mon, Derek," Max said, "we're across, and that's all that matters." He got up as they both looked again at the towering fruit tree now in front of them. Its massive branches cast a shadow over them all.

"Okay, so now you can tell us, exactly what is this?" Max asked, circling closer to touch the mossy, wet surface of the giant form.

"It's… well, it's hard to explain."

"Is it alive? Down here?"

"Sort of."

"How can it be 'sort of' alive?"

"Because it is a tree of life, one that was, shall we say 'borrowed'?"

"You mean stolen!" Derek stared at the massive structure and looked back at Humphries.

"I wasn't part of that deal, it was before my time, but let's say some folks are upset about it still."

"How could anything even resembling a tree live down here?"

Max scowled for a moment, biting tightly against his bottom lip. "Wait, Derek. It makes perfect sense. It can live here because the very substance it stores is time—in other words, life itself." Max turned toward Humphries. "These pipes in the ground, are these what the Boggarts use to empty their Time Extractors?"

"Quite right, Max. These pipes lead directly to the tree's root system, which absorbs the time they collected. It then passes through to the apples and transforms inside them into the highest concentration of life force possible: prana."

"I bet they're great tasting, then!!" Derek said, smacking his lips. "Oh man! And they're giant size! C'mon, Max, I'm starving. We've got to find a way to shinny up this thing and grab some of those."

"Not so fast," Max cautioned, "we first need to stop Abaddon."

"But how are you going to do that? Even if you stop him from emptying the Vault, he's just going to keep making more of this stuff," said Sam. "We would have to find a way to stop all of this," she said, gesturing with her arm to the entire tree.

"That's just it, you don't need to stop it all, just that!" Humphries said, pointing off to a stone cottage building to the side of the massive tree.

Max and Derek both squinted to make out the object Humphries was pointing to.

"What? I don't see anything but an old farm building," Derek complained.

"That's not any old farm building, Derek," Humphries said in almost a whisper. "That's a press!"

"You mean like a printing press?"

"No! Like a fruit press!" Max said, with sudden realization.

Humphries nodded. "The tree transfers the time energy into the apples, but it's the press that squeezes it out, and makes it into…"

"Apple cider! Even better!"

"No—prana, you goof!" Sam replied.

By this time, Max, Derek, and Humphries had slowly circled the tall tree and stood on its opposite side. Next to the stone cottage that housed the press stood a big metal bin, resembling a large upside-down pyramid.

"And that's the hopper where they load the fruit, before it feeds into the press," Max said. "Right?"

Humphries was impressed at how quickly Max had grasped the process. "Yes, the Gargons actually harvest the fruit from the tree and place it in the hopper where it gets squeezed into pure—"

Derek stopped Humphries mid-sentence. "'Gargons'? Wait, don't tell me… The freakish sized spider-things that drop out of nowhere and shoot crazy web strings all over."

"Wait, how do you know about Gargons?" Humphries asked, puzzled.

"Let's just say they took us for a spin," Sam said, snidely.

"Well then you know, they're like a cross between a large spider and a leech. They spin web baskets to catch the falling apples and use their suction cups to carry them over and drop them in this hopper for processing. We don't get near them much since all we Boggarts do is empty our Extractors down those feeding pipes," he said pointing at the angled tubes surrounding the tree.

"But are Gargons dangerous?"

"It depends. They've never bothered a Boggart. But then again, they've never had reason to."

"Humphries, back to the press!" Max interrupted, flashing his growing impatience. "Where does all the processed liquid—the prana—go, where is it all stored? You said that over there was the Vault."

"Right! Right!" Humphries pointed up to the cone-shaped stone structure, the one resembling a volcano.

Derek craned his neck for a better look. "All that goo gets dumped in there?"

"You make it sound like it's some sort of toxin. This is good stuff, pure life energy. Fleshies would die for this. And it doesn't 'dump' into a volcano. It's piped from the press into the inside, where it sits right over a geothermal hot spot, where it's superheated."

"You mean it gets boiled?"

"Pretty much, that's what condenses it down to the purest form."

"What's to keep it from overheating and spewing out?"

"It's plugged at the top with a brimstone lid—a rather big one, I might add. Keeps it sealed that way, can't flow out and no one can break in. That's why they call it—"

"The Vault!" Max shouted in amazement. "Of course!"

"Exactly. But no ordinary vault, mind you. This one's built specifically to store time. It's strong enough to seal in 500 billion years of *prana* and seal out all the inhabitants of Nemesis."

"Why all the bother?" asked Derek. "Why not just squeeze out a bunch of apple cider and call it a day?"

"It's the only way that time can be accumulated without spoiling," said Humphries, growing visibly impatient with Derek's questions. "The *prana* in those Extractors is only good for a short time, then it vaporizes. And the 'cider,' as you call it, would go bad as well. In order to save up that much time, it has to be liquefied, pressurized, and heated. Hey, I don't make the rules, it's just the way it works."

Derek nodded. "So when does all this prana stuff come spewing out?"

"Judging by all the activity, I would guess anytime now. Once the Vault is full, the pressure will automatically blow the lid off, and the prana will come streaming out through underground pipes and right into the waiting hungry mouths of everyone gathering right now in the Assembly. The first thing they will transform is themselves to enter your world, every Wereboard, Nark, Barghest, Changeling, Hobgoblin you can imagine, eating and feasting their way through the lives of everyone you know. Every human and every animal."

"But then there will be nothing left," Sam said in horror, thinking of both her dad and her cat, Mt. Jitters.

"For them it's the energy in human life forms that they're after, like a quick fuel stop, they can double up on you humans, drain you and drop you, and then move on. It's that simple."

"A fuel stop? To go where?" Derek asked.

"Where they ultimately want to go… back to Empyrean!"

CHAPTER 30

"The way I see it," Max said, "we have two main objectives." Using the end of a Time Extractor, he drew a diagram in the ground. "We have to empty the Vault and then take out this press. Once the Vault is emptied, they can't invade our world. And once the press is gone, they can't process any more prana."

"But what about the tree?" asked Derek.

"Without the press, they can't make the condensed prana, the kind they need to power through," Humphries agreed. "Besides, I wouldn't mess with a tree of life, it's bad karma. And that's coming from a Boggart."

"But how can we possibly do all that?" Derek asked, his voice rising. "There's just the four of us, and the Assembly is getting ready to start any time now. And what about objective three—getting back home?"

Max shook his head. "If we don't at least empty the Vault, there won't be a home worth going to. You think I want to stay here any more than you do? The fact is that time is literally running out, and we've got to do whatever we can."

"And fast," Humphries added.

"I know, I know…" Derek slumped down on a misshapen rock, one of many that ringed the perimeter of the massive tree.

"Humphries… don't you have any other friends down here?" Max inquired.

"Friends?" He laughed bitterly. "Not after being so long in jail. A few dropped by at first. Besides, even if they wanted to help me, why would they want to empty the Vault? Sorry, Max, I'm no help on that one."

"There must be someone… or someway," Max murmured to himself. He scanned the area for any sign of life, but all he could see was the glowing fruit above and the rock-strewn floor below.

"Why are all these rocks piled around the tree? To protect it?" Derek asked Humphries. "It's not like someone would drive a car through here and hit the tree."

"I'm not sure," Humphries replied. "They weren't here the last time I was here, but then again, that was hundreds of years ago."

"Yeah, and there must be over a hundred of these things," Derek said, sliding off of one and into another.

Max touched one, then another, feeling their smoothness. They had an almost statue-like appearance, some more upright than others. Derek busied himself by making an exact count. "One hundred and twenty-five," he said proudly. "Oops… I forgot the one I'm sitting on now. That would make it one hundred twenty-six."

"Derek! Do you mind? I'm trying to concentrate here; you need to pay attention to what's going on," Max demanded, but Derek's ADD had kicked in and he was busy hopping on and off the odd-shaped stones.

"Yep! One hundred twenty-six, almost the exact number of those miniature marshmallows I ate during that fourth grade Halloween party in Mr. Muller's class. Remember how I puked in that kid's backpack? He sat at the desk in front of me. Wait, I think it was Kyle! His stepmom got all mad and called my folks. What were their names?"

"Wait," said Max, "I think it might be the monks!"

"No, it wasn't the Monks," Derek said, "but I think you're close. The Monroes… The Morgans…"

"No! Remember? There were one hundred twenty-six monks who came here! In the manuscript? Don't you find that a weird coincidence?"

"Yes," Sam agreed, "that seems way more than a coincidence," as she grabbed the manuscript and rifled through its pages.

"Find what a coincidence? We are talking about rocks, aren't we?"

Max turned quickly to Humphries. "Whatever happened to the monks? You never said."

"All I was told was that they were 'dealt with,'" Humphries said with a shudder. "That usually means the Abyss."

"Is there any other form of punishment down here?" Max asked intently.

"Well, sure, all sorts. There's Nark drags, Wereboar stomps, Hobgoblin feedings, Gargon wraps…"

"Gargon wraps? What are those?"

"I've never witnessed one, but Gargons are very protective of the tree, so they'll stop at nothing to defend it. That includes casting a web around any intruder and spinning them inside a permanent cocoon."

Max knocked on one of the stones with his knuckles. A deep hollow sound echoed off the surrounding walls. He held his ear closer and knocked again.

"What are you doing, Max?" Derek asked in exasperation. "I thought you said we were in a hurry. What do these rocks have to do with anything?"

"Those just might not be rocks," Sam said, watching Max at work.

"Agreed," Max stated matter-of-factly. Then he calmly picked up one of the Time Extractors and *BAM!*—smashed the barrel stock against the solid rock surface where Derek sat.

"Have you gone crazy? Max, you're going to wreck one of the few weapons we have left!"

BAM! Max slammed the Extractor again. This time a cracking sound rang out.

"Great! Now you've busted it!" Derek moaned.

"Yeah, I busted something, but it's not the gun." Derek looked at the "rock" underneath him. A small fissure had opened up, revealing a hollow core inside.

"Humphries, quick! Use your Extractor light to shine in there. Derek, Sam, each of you grab one side of this thing and pull hard. I'll grab the other." The crack in the "rock" suddenly opened wider, allowing for a look inside. Carefully, the four stepped closer, and Humphries shined his Extractor light around, probing the interior.

"What th—?" Before Derek could finish, the crack instantly widened farther and the contents inside of the "rock" fell out with a thud.

"It's a freakin' mummy!" Derek shrieked, almost jumping into Humphries' many arms.

"Not quite," Max stated calmly. "I believe it's a monk." He turned the Time Extractor over on its end, flipped the switch to green, and let loose a jagged bolt of energy. The mummy-like form was jolted, thrusting from side to side. Max hit it again.

"Aaahhhrrgghh!"

The scream sounded sharply. *"Dépêchez-vous! Arrêtez-eux! Nous devons les arrêter!"*

"Quick! Grab a set of those Boggart clippers and cut him loose!" Max shouted.

"Even better," Humphries insisted, using one of his long sharp fingernails to cut a V-shaped opening in the tight netting encasing the "mummy." The limp figure rolled over to one side, revealing a thin, drawn-out face that seemed frozen and expressionless. It sat for a moment, then the mouth moved slowly.

"Qu'est-ce qui se passe? Où suis-je?"

"Man, I wish we had that Latin translation program here," Derek said. "Who knows what he's saying…"

"It's *French*," Max insisted. "Something you would know if you didn't sleep through French class! The monks were from France, remember?"

"Okay, okay. So what's he saying?"

"He just asked what's going on and where are we," Sam said.

The "mummy" now looked at Max and said in an imploring voice, *"Pardon? Que voulez-vous dire?"*

"Okay, I'll let you two handle this," Derek said to Max. "And I'll just stand over on this rock and see if I can reach one of those apples."

Max collected his thoughts before speaking. His French came out haltingly.

"Sam, can you help?"

"Sure," she said, concentrating for a moment. "Vous êtes dans un endroit appelé Nemesis. Vous êtes venus ici pour vider la chambre forte."

"What did you tell him?" asked Derek, jumping at the low hanging fruit.

"I said we're in a place called Nemesis and we came here to empty the vault."

"The Vault?" echoed the "mummy."

"He speaks English!" Derek shouted in disbelief.

Max rolled his eyes. "He was just repeating what I said, you doofus! You actually think a five-hundred year-old monk from France knows a word of English?"

"I speak some," the monk replied in a thick accent. "My name… my name is Johannes Chanoteau, leader of the Cluniac and Benedictine monks at the University of Paris. Where are my brothers? Are they all right?"

Derek gloated, "See, I told you both! Everyone knows English!"

"Your brothers?" Max said to the monk, ignoring Derek. "You mean your fellow monks? I believe they're all here in these stones. The Gargons sealed you up in these cocoons. The outside shells must have slowly petrified over the past five hundred years."

"So, we did not defeat Abaddon's army?"

"Well, you stopped them somehow, but Abaddon is planning to attack again, this time with a lot more force."

"But how did you find your way here? Where is the manuscript?"

"Right here!" Sam replied, holding it up high, like a prized trophy.

"Plus, we had help," Max said, pointing to Humphries.

"A Boggart? You were helped by a Boggart?" Johannes stared at Humphries in disbelief. "Well, apparently some things have changed. Quickly, we don't have much time. We must free my other men."

"Here—take one of these." Max handed a Time Extractor to Johannes. "Hit the outside firmly and it should crack. Then flip this switch, pull the trigger, and aim inside. With about two good shots, it should restore enough life force to make them conscious again." Max used the blunt end of his Extractor to demonstrate on the next big stone. The outside shell of it cracked, revealing another mummified monk. Max fired two shots and the figure contorted, rolled around for a second and then sat up, hands fighting the webbing around it.

"Faites moi sortir d'ici!"

"Paschal!" Johannes cried, falling to his knees to embrace his second-in-command. "And yes, we'll get you out of here. Hold on, help has arrived. I can't explain now but do as these gentlemen tell you. First, we must free all our brothers."

Once fully awakened and informed of the situation, Paschal, along with Derek and Sam worked their way along the perimeter, alternately cracking open the hard shells with the butt of their Extractors, reactivating the men inside with jolts from the guns, and freeing them from their webbed bondage. Max and Johannes teamed up to work in the other direction. As each man was freed from the shelled casings, Johannes quickly embraced him, explaining the situation and then providing instructions to help the others.

"What is your given name, if I may ask?" said Johannes as they worked to free the last of the remaining men.

"Max. Max Kellerman."

Johannes bowed deeply. "Sir Max, I cannot thank you enough for what you've done. Where are the rest of your men? Are they in hiding?"

"You're looking at them."

"The four of you?" Johannes said in a startled voice, almost missing the stone he was cracking. "And with only the manuscript? Surely you must have had other aid."

"Well, I met a professor who told me about this place," Max told Johannes. "He gave me the manuscript. That's how I found out about you. It turns out you stopped the famines and plagues. Things actually got better, thanks to you."

"It wasn't me, Max. I also had a teacher, but he was from a place far from here. His name was…"

Max stopped still. "Wait! Don't tell me, you've met Zadkiel, too?"

"Yes, I know him well. It was our life's work to seek the unseen, to know the unknowable. And in some of those quiet moments back in the monastery, deep in meditation, he would appear. That's how we found out about this place. That's why we came here."

"Hey! They're all freed!" Derek shouted. "What should we do now?"

"Max, one thing you should know about this place," Johannes cautioned. "They play on your fears. They use your own mind as a weapon against you."

"Yeah, I've sort of found that out myself the hard way—"

"Hey, Max! What's the hold up?" Derek interrupted.

KKRRAACCCKKOOOWW!

Suddenly the ground beneath their feet shook violently. A sound like rolling thunder swept through the vast chamber. "The Vault!" Humphries screamed. "The lid is blowing!"

The ground under their feet began to shake violently, and with each sweeping motion, the glowing, grapefruit size apples above them began raining on their heads.

"Ow! Those suckers hurt!" Derek cried.

"Quick! There's no time! Back into the tunnels! The Assembly's about to start," shouted Humphries.

"But what about the tree?" Max shouted over the roar of the rumbling Vault.

"I don't think that's going to be an issue, Max," Humphries yelled back as he scrambled for the tunnel entrance. "The Vault has never held this much pure prana. I don't think the distribution tubes can handle the molten energy coming this way! If not, this whole place is going up!"

An ear-shattering crash filled the room. The massive stone lid to the Vault blew straight up, then breaking into large fragments, showered down around them, one flaming chunk smashing down an arm's length from Derek.

"Holy—"

"Watch out, Derek!" Max threw himself hard against Derek, knocking him to the ground. A second piece of the brimstone lid crashed directly where Derek had just stood and buried itself several inches into the ground.

Derek slowly got back up. "Wow… now that was close. Thanks, Max… Max?"

"Look!" Sam shouted, pointing back up to the summit of the Vault.

Max's gaze was already fixed on the now open throat of the Vault. What looked like a hot flow of bright magma was pouring down the sides.

"You're right about the Vault," Max yelled to Humphries, as the entire group of stunned onlookers watched a fiery river of thick molten *prana* stream down the side of the Vault, entering the tops of several large tubes, but also overflowing them, and heading in their direction!

"Come, Max! Let's get out of here!" Derek yelled.

"There's no use in staying, Max," Johannes agreed. "We must get to the Assembly. It will be minutes before the prana comes out the distribution tubes and into the Assembly. We must find a way to stop it before it cools enough for everyone waiting in there to drink it."

Max watched as the leading edge of the fiery overflowing mixture reached the roots of the large tree. But instead of burning like normal wood, the tree seemed to absorb the flow, soaking it in and transforming into the same purple color and texture of the mixture itself. Soon the entire trunk and branches seemed ablaze in the *prana* energy.

"Max! Now!" Derek pleaded. Max turned back one more time to see the tree growing brighter and brighter until at once it collapsed into the very force that consumed it.

What just happened? Max wondered as the group hurried off. *What just died?* In place of the towering tree lay a shimmering pool, and in the reflection, Max could see his own distorted image. The way to live longer, the way to stabilize time and to store life itself was now gone. Whether good or bad, Max felt a sudden sadness, as if a piece of history had just vanished forever. He let out a troubled sigh, then turned to join the others.

"Wait! The ridge! It's gone, remember!" Max called out ahead to the group. But they were already aware, huddled up tight against the ledge that separated them from the tunnels that led back to the Assembly floor.

"No problem, Max," Johannes replied, "I had each man bring the Gargon web he was wrapped in, just in case we needed it." With that, he tossed a long strand attached to a thin, oblong rock. The rock caught in a crevice above, and with a couple of hard pulls, Johannes turned back to Max. "There, it held. We should be able to swing back across."

"Great!" Max said, appreciative of the quick thinking. "Humphries, put Sam and Derek on your back to save time; let's see if we can go three to four each trip." Within minutes the group regathered on the other ledge, just outside the tunnel that led into the Assembly.

"Shhhh!" Humphries cautioned Max. "We're at the final corner that turns back to the Assembly… the same way we came out. Everyone, and I mean everyone, is in there."

Max could hear the muffled roar of a massive throng. The place reverberated with excitement.

"They are in rare form," Humphries whispered. "Imagine waiting six hundred years for an event like this."

"Like waiting for the Red Sox to win another World Series?" Derek agreed.

"Okay, so we need a plan," Max said. He looked over to Johannes and asked, "Just exactly how did you guys pull this off the last time?"

"Pull this off?"

"Sorry," Max said, and then rephrased the question. "How did you empty the Vault?"

"Oh, it took some effort," Johannes recalled. "At first, we just hid for a long time in order to study their methods. We had the advantage of the manuscript as well. Once we understood how the time was processed and where it was stored, it was just a matter of removing the lid and draining the Vault."

"But where did you drain it? Where can time go where no one can recover it?" Max asked.

"Into the Abyss itself," replied Johannes. "We found out just when they were planning to do the Transformation, the last one, and we hid one man near the entrance of the Assembly. He ran out into the middle of it, knowing they would take him and throw him into the Abyss. Just as they opened it to throw him in, we got word, and removed the lid to the Vault, it took everything we had to move it. The *prana* started flowing down the distribution tubes, which we had re-routed to flow right toward the Abyss, and that's precisely where it went."

"Boy, I bet Abaddon was pissed!" Derek laughed.

"Pissed?"

"Ignore him," Max advised Johannes. "So, what happened next?"

"Well, first it reactivated everything that had been thrown into that Abyss."

"Talk about all hell breaking loose," Derek said with surprise.

"Yes, it was sheer madness, and Abaddon sent all his armies to seek us out. We knew he was coming for us, so we circled the tree to prepare for the final attack. All we had were a handful of those things you call…"

"Extractors?" Sam offered.

"Yes, yes those. And that's the last I remember."

"But why didn't you just take out the tree? You were right there, standing around it with Extractors!" Derek asked.

"We couldn't do it even if we knew how," Johannes replied.

"Why?" asked Humphries, curious as well.

"The tree represents something very special, very old. It never belonged here. It was stolen millennia ago. Our charge was to keep Abaddon from breaking through to Earth, but we were never to destroy that which both informs and transforms life itself."

"Well, now that the tree is out of the picture, we're all set, right?" Derek asked. "I mean the *prana* will just come shooting out of those distribution tubes, we use the same playbook and direct it right into the Abyss and *bam!*—it's all over."

"Not quite," said Humphries. "They know better than to open it now before the Transformation; they won't make that same mistake twice."

"Your Boggart friend is right, Derek. We caught Nemesis by surprise, knowing they were already in a feeding frenzy. A human sacrifice was too tempting to pass up."

"Well, that's just great!" Derek exclaimed in disgust. "The tree that you and your monk buddies were supposed to protect is now toast, and the crazies in there are about to be beamed into our backyards. And from what you're telling us, there's nothing we can do to stop it, no plan A or B?"

"We did all that we could do," Johannes replied sadly.

"Wait!" Humphries whispered in excitement. "It's Abaddon. He's about to address the Assembly. Listen!"

From their position in the Boggart tunnel, just under the main Assembly, they could hear what sounded like a slow, drawn out, almost hissing voice. The sound itself sent a cold chill up Max's spine, as if the voice entered through the ground itself and traveled up through every vertebra in his back, lodging in the very forefront of his mind.

"Inhabitants of Nemesis! We have waited long for this moment in time… this moment of destiny. Soon you will be feeding on the *prana* harvested from tens of millions of unsuspecting fleshies, whose world you will now be able to enter, where you will be able to feast directly, to your heart's content. Remember, your journey is only now beginning, so spare no one or no thing. Store up by devouring all you can, whatever moves, there is no room for weakness, no time for mercy.

"Are you getting this, Max? That means your mom, my parents, Sam's dad…"

Max could feel his fist tightening. *First these monks, then my father and Professor Gutt, and now everyone and everything that's left in my life… this has got to end.*

"With Earth destroyed, you will finally take your place as the rightful rulers of the mortal realm. There will be no more living in the shadows, no more fleeting glimpses of reality. We will at last reign as kings on Earth! And once we have secured our place, we will be one step closer to our ultimate destiny as rulers of all worlds… all levels, as the Lords of Empyrean itself!"

"Max! We've got to do something," Sam pleaded, visibly shaken by the voice and the destruction it foretold. "My dad and cat are all I have besides you two," she said, her own voice now trembling with emotion.

"Listen!" Humphries insisted.

He had his ear up to the tunnel wall. A gurgling sound could be heard from somewhere deep inside. "The *prana* in the distribution tubes is slowing down, it must almost be cooled," he said. "It's about to flow into the Assembly, then into the feeding troughs."

"Humphries, you said Abaddon has control over the Abyss, correct?" Max asked. "Abbaddon and Mephisto. Is there anyone else? Any other way?"

"Abaddon can do it at will, Mephisto with permission. The only other way requires something that quit working eons ago."

"The Seven Eyes of Empyrean," Johannes said in amazement.

"That's just it," said Humprhies, "it's the Six Eyes right now, one went missing, there's a hole in the wall where it—"

"Yeah!" Sam chimed in with growing excitement. "I remember seeing a rough drawing in the manuscript. It looked like seven fragments that fit together like some kind of puzzle, with some scribbles on each of them; it was hard to tell just what they were from the drawings. Why? Are you thinking the missing Eye could be—"

"Zadkiel's stone!" Max motioned, removing Zekdiel's stone from under his shirt and around his neck, holding it up high.

Humphries' eyes widened in terror while Johannes drew near for closer inspection.

"Yes, Max, I believe that could be it!" Johannes remarked in amazement.

"Max, for the love of Boggarts, put that away!" Humphries stammered.

"Zadkiel told me about it, said it's part of something bigger."

"You think it can bypass Abbadon's will and open the Abyss?" Johannes asked, now holding the object like a sought-after diamond.

"Maybe," said Max. "It's just a matter of getting into the Assembly and giving it a try, right? If it works, we can set off some of those Boggart detonators, empty everyone out of the Assembly, and with no one there to drink the prana, it will flow back into the Abyss, just like last time."

"That's crazy, Max!" Derek protested. "Did you forget about the head honcho in there? Abaddon? He's not just going to let you waltz in and pop open the Abyss with a mystery rock. There's got to be a better plan."

"Listen, Derek, listen closely," Max insisted. "There is no Plan B, this is it! Do you hear that? It's *Prana*! It's flowing in there as we speak. If I don't at least try to open the Abyss, then we've come all this way for nothing."

"Max," Johannes said, "what if my men and I were to create some sort of diversion, something to draw Abaddon's attention away from the Assembly while you attempt to open the Abyss?"

"It would have to be huge to interrupt this final production," said Humphries. "Abaddon's not about to leave to chase a few intruders away during the Transformation."

"Forget chasing a few runaway intruders," Max said, "let's see how he deals with a flying traffic jam."

"Pray, what do you have in mind, Sir Max?" asked Johannes.

"Humphries, where are the Narks kept?"

"In a set of stables, no more than a Wereboar toss from here, farther down this tunnel, in fact. What are you thinking, Max?"

"You said that Narks automatically seek out intruders and scoop them up, correct?"

"Yes?" Humphries replied hesitantly.

"Johannes, take Paschal and your men and follow Humphries to the Nark stables. Sam, go with them; let every Nark loose that you can. Derek, come with me. We've got some time to kill—and there's not a second to waste."

CHAPTER 31

"**D**rink! Drink deeply!" came a laughing voice that resounded throughout the Assembly chamber. The rodent-like faces of the Assembly members drooled in anxious expectation of the *prana* as it emerged from the distribution tubes and slogged down the rough rock troughs in front of them. There sat all manner of inhabitants of Nemesis, from the largest Barghest imaginable to the tiniest Hobgoblin, nibbling at the feet of a group of Boggarts. Even the magistrate from the jail and the cricket receptionist were on hand, eagerly bent over the troughs to get the first possible gulp.

"To Abaddon!" a Barghest shouted, scooping a cupful of the slushy, fluorescent substance as it sluiced down the trough, and holding it high as it dripped through his scaly fingers in salute.

"To Abaddon!" the hordes shouted in loyal obedience.

"Max, what now? It's too late, they're drinking the prana, the monks haven't made it back." Max squirmed, looked back over the Assembly walls and seeing nothing, abruptly stood up.

"To Abaddon!" he announced to the utter shock and surprise of all the Assembly.

"Praise be to him! Thief of all time! Hoarder of life! Keeper of the *prana*! Go ahead and toast him—talk of his exploits, speak of his power, and then drink of his lies."

Derek turned sheet white, falling back on his heels, head reeling.

"Max... what have you done! We're dead meat now!" Derek's eyes pleaded for a different reality, but he knew full well what he had just witnessed. He remained crouched tight and low, wedged behind a stone column which Max had mounted to make his bold proclamation.

"It's the only way, Derek," Max shouted down in a hoarse whisper to his frightened friend. "We can't win by running. We have to face him. I have to face him."

What light there was in the Assembly suddenly shut off, the entire arena fell pitch-black. The bustling throng grew eerily quiet, with only murmurs and hushed whispers rippling through the crowd. Max could see nothing, not even the hand in front of his face.

"Psst, Max! What's happening?" Derek whispered.

"I'm not sure." Max tried desperately to adjust to the dense blackness of the Assembly chamber. "I can't see anything."

"You can't see anything because there's nothing to see." The voice came so close he felt its breath sweep across his face, a breath that reeked of rot and decay. Max felt the hairs on the back of his neck stand up. He stretched out his hands, frantically feeling, searching for anything that might be there, but all he sensed was the close, moist stench of the invisible presence.

"Were you so naïve, Max, to think I didn't know you were here? Did you think I would just let you storm in here—you, a worthless fleshie—and destroy everything I've planned?"

"I know all about your plan!" Max snapped back at the faceless figure. "And I know it will never work!"

"But Max, it already has! Don't you see? As long as there was the manuscript and someone who knew how to use it, there was a chance we might fail. But you've assured our success! You were our best hope, and now both you and the manuscript are here, right in the middle of Assembly, right in time for the Transformation, delivered just as planned. Right, Humphries?"

Max felt Humphries' body shoved into his, knocking him to the ground. "I'm sorry, Max!" came the muffled cry as Barghests bound and began to gag him. "It was the only way I could ever earn my freedom." Max felt his muscles collapse as his heart sank—as if all the blood in his body had suddenly and permanently drained out. He struggled to get back on his feet.

"Humphries??!!" Max stammered, still in disbelief, taking two to three steps back. "But why?? Why would you... we rescued you! We let you out of prison... and *trusted* you!!"

"Ha!" Abaddon bellowed in dark laughter. "You sealed your fate by coming here, Max—you and the rest of your world with it."

"Why don't you come out here then," Max shouted defiantly. "Show your face, you coward!" Max felt blindly in the darkness for the Time Extractor around his back, and finding it, pointed it aimlessly forward. "C'mon! Show me what you're made of!"

"That's just it, Max, I already have. I'm the very darkness that surrounds you. I'm what fills this place, creates its shadows, and dims the lights. I've been here since the beginning, and you just didn't know it. And now for the final part of the plan…"

Max felt a cold grip around his throat, raising him a few inches off his feet. The touch of icy fingers touched his chest, finding Zadkiels' stone, then forcefully ripping it off from around his neck.

"You see, Max, you were definitely a part of the plan. You wonder if your life has purpose, and I assure you it does—fulfilling mine! You see, you have the only missing piece of tablet, the last and most important piece! The emerald Eye of Empyrean, the one that opens the gate, you had that right. But not the gate to the Abyss, the gate to our freedom, the gate to your world above, the gate to the worlds beyond!"

With one swift motion, the fragment disappeared into the thick blackness. Almost instantly a dim glow appeared on the far side of the Assembly floor, faint at first, then growing in brilliance. Max could make out what looked like a circular ring, a display of gem-like stones, three to a side, embedded in the wall just above the Abyss. All six of the stones had a different color gem in its center. In the middle sat a vacant space, as if waiting to be filled.

"This is *not* good, Max!" Derek whispered frantically behind him. "That stone was our last hope…"

Suddenly, the entire Assembly arena lit up.

"Look!" Derek exclaimed. "Abaddon must have put that last piece in place!" Max could clearly see the entire ring of gemstones, now seven in total, with Zadkiel's stone in the middle, radiating a bright greenish white light. As the gemstones all glowed in unison, their light began to meld into one bold, brilliant beam of light. The powerful ray intensified until it shot straight up from the center of the ring to the Assembly ceiling at what appeared to be a large metal seal, like the wax seal on a letter, but made of something much harder.

"Let the seal be broken!" Abaddon announced to another throng of wild cheers. A slow cracking sound reverberated throughout the chamber as the seal began to melt from the heat of the brilliant light.

CRASH!

As the seal melted away, two huge gate doors swung loose with a *swoosh*, swinging back and forth under their immense weight. Where the sealed doors once hung in the ceiling above, now revealed a wide opening, a beckoning portal cloaked in a deep purple darkness and extending out of sight. The air in the room rushed upwards as if beckoning all to follow.

"Aaarrggghh!" the Assembly of Nemesis roared in delight.

"Eat! Eat and ascend!" Abaddon commanded them. Eagerly, the masses gulped, slurped, and gorged themselves with *prana*, fighting and clawing at each other in an effort to rise and transcend first.

Slowly, one by one, creatures lifted skyward. A Changeling here, a Barghest there, several Wereboars, tusks flashing in excitement, all ascending toward the now open gates.

"See, Max! See how much you have helped our cause! They are now entering your world, thanks to you—you and your father. Your father failed, and now you. Failure must be a proud family tradition. Tonight, this army will turn every child's dream into nightmares as they emerge to take control of your pathetic little planet."

Max felt a surge of rage shoot through his body. Grabbing the Time Extractor, he shot directly at the glowing tablet of stone.

"Max, don't!" yelled Derek, emerging from his hiding place behind the pedestal. "It's no use, just run!"

"Your little friend is right, Max, it won't work! The only thing that can be extracted now is your own life." All at once Max felt the Time Extractor fly out of his hands, only to appear again directly in front of him, floating in space, pointed right at his eyes.

"You were wrong, Max, wrong all along. Your whole life has been a search for purpose, hasn't it, Max? And you thought this was it! Unlock the Abyss and drain the *prana*. Ha-ha-ha! But all you unlocked was the gate to our freedom." Max looked to see the first few creatures now nearing the top of the ceiling, just entering the gates, their greedy hands waving goodbye to those below.

Instinctively Max pushed the Extractor away from his face and ran full tilt toward the glowing tablet, intent to take back Zadkiel's stone.

"You'll never make it," laughed Abaddon, as the Time Extractor turned and floated behind him, tracing his every step.

"Max! Look out!" Derek screamed in warning. But it was too late. The Extractor's jagged bolt hit Max squarely in the back.

"AAAHHHH!!!!" Max cried out in pain.

"Do you feel that, Max?" Abaddon roared with laughter. "That's the feeling of emptiness—the feeling of every moment of your pathetic, meaningless life, every memory and belief you've ever held, all evaporating away. Soon there will be nothing left of you Mr. Max Kellerman but a story, and a sad one at that."

Wincing in pain, Max moved toward the glowing stone, determined to reach it no matter what. With each step forward, he felt a strange fuzziness and confusion. Thoughts of his parents flashed through his mind and vanished.

ZZAAMM!! Another bolt rang through him, this one several times longer than the last.

He could no longer recall where he was from, or people he had known. Someone behind him was yelling for him to stop and turn back, to run. They kept waving wildly, but he only felt the need to keep moving ahead, as if by sheer momentum. *Moving... just keep moving,* he told himself. His thoughts grew further and further apart. He now stood in front of the glowing stone and yet could think of nothing to do.

Am I dead? he wondered.

"Depends on what you mean by dead," came the reply.

Max turned to see a tall, bearded figure standing at his side. "Who are you?"

"It doesn't really matter at this point. The more important question is who are you?"

"I'm not sure. I mean, I don't remember."

"Do you need to remember to know who you are? Do you need words and labels to define yourself?"

Max paused and slowly looked up into the eyes of the bearded man. There was something vaguely familiar about him. His weathered face seemed etched with kindness, but Max couldn't place the face or recall the name.

"All that I know for sure is that I'm here, in this moment," said Max.

The gentle worn eyes in front of Max softened even more, they looked deeply into Max's own eyes as if imparting a message.

"Then perhaps that's all you need to know."

The large figure nodded at Max, as if in acknowledgment, and then faded into the whiteness that surrounded him.

In the twilight that followed, Max could make out what appeared to be a body, much like his own, lying face down just inches away from a wall with a glowing ring of gemstones. Someone had run up to the body, yelling, screaming, hugging it, cradling it in his arms, and sobbing deeply. Max felt sorry for whoever this person was that was so saddened by the loss of his friend. Max reached out to help but his own hand passed right through both of them.

"Who are you! I killed you! You are supposed to be dead, lifeless, gone! Why is your presence still here?" demanded the voice.

"I don't know," Max replied.

"But there's your body!" came the angry voice, now pointing to where Derek lay hugging the limp outline of a figure.

Max saw a darkness surrounding him but felt nothing. The darkness engulfed him and swirled around him.

"Have you no idea what I am capable of!" the voice of Abaddon shrieked in rage. "I will kill everything you love, everything you value! Everything!!" Pictures flashed in front of Max, images of people and places, but they meant nothing to him. "Don't you know what this is? It's your very life and I will continue to destroy it. I will enter your world and cripple all you have ever known or touched! I alone control Nemesis and now I will control your world! You cannot remain, do you understand!"

"Go?" Max replied. "I can only be where I am," he replied calmly, not understanding the wrath in his voice. "I am here, and for now that's all I know." Max approached the darkness, and it recoiled instinctively. Sensing something odd, something foreign, Max leaned in, now staring deeply in the face of Abaddon himself. "You seem afraid," he said. "Is there anything I can do to help you?"

"AFRAID!! ME!! I fear nothing!" the voice shrieked. "I AM fear! How dare you mock me!" The dark outline of Abaddon began to shift and distort, slowly changing appearances, from a gnarled Wereboar to a heinous Changeling.

"I am many things, all sorts of things," the voice heightened in intensity, rifling through more identities, searching for the deadliest one. Finally, it settled into the shape of a long black spear, like a medieval lance forged from fire and glistening in the dim light. The fearsome weapon grew sharper and more vivid in detail. Razor tipped and menacing, it now floated in place, aimed directly at Max's heart.

"Maybe your body didn't respond, but what little remains of you, Max, will finally taste what true suffering is!" and with that, the black spear recoiled, thrusting itself directly at Max, passing right through him seamlessly, effortlessly.

Max felt nothing. No impact, no pain. The force of Abaddon's energy carried the dark instrument of destruction through the nothingness that now defined Max—a body without time, a body without memory, a body without resistance. Tightly bound and blind to his own rage, Abaddon's embodied spear found no physical target to hit, nothing tangible to destroy. Sailing through the essence of Max, he came speeding out the other side, and unable to stop himself, crashed wildly into the glowing ring of gemstones. The sheer impact shattered the prized ring, knocking all seven gemstones loose and scattering them in different directions.

AHHHHHHH!!! came the shrieks as the huge gate doors on the ceiling above began to swing back shut. Several Barghest and two Wereboars that were just about to clear the gates got crushed in between them, sealing the doors and their fate.

Max looked down to see the person next to him still holding the body of his friend. A large six-legged creature walked up to the grieving victim.

"This is all your fault!" the grieving friend screamed at the three-eyed creature. "Max and I trusted you and you betrayed us! I told him we should never have trusted you… I told him and now look! I hope you rot down here forever! You and your mutant Boggart friends!"

The strange creature simply stood there before finally leaning over and grasping the Time Extractor lying on the chamber floor. He picked it up and aimed directly at them.

"So now what? You're gonna zap me? Just like Abaddon did to him! Go ahead, Humphries! Go ahead and see if I care. Just do it!"

A jagged bolt blazed the air, missing Derek completely and piercing the body that Derek held onto.

ZZAAMM!! Max suddenly felt a jolt. *What's happening? What are these strange feelings?* A swirl of images began flooding his mind—people, places, events. "Wait… I have a mom? Where am I? Nemesis? I've got to get out of here, I've gotta help my friends! Dad!" With the second blast of energy came a flood of emotions. Max felt himself choking and gasping for life.

"Wait," he thought. "Am I…"

"Max! You're alive!" Derek's face flooded with tears. "Oh my gosh, you're alive! You are one freak of nature!" he said, grabbing Max forcefully by the shoulders and shaking him wildly. "Are you alright?"

"Other than a splitting headache and the whiplash you just gave me, I think I'll survive," Max replied. It was good—no, great!—to see Derek again. Max felt a renewed and deep appreciation for his friendship. Max paused for a moment to collect himself when he saw a familiar set of six feet standing beside him.

"You know, I think I must have entered the code for this very little-known option on the Extractor and hit him with some high-quality prana," Humphries explained. "It pays sometimes to be a Master Boggart. Although I was never much good at following rules."

"Look, Humphries," Max said, looking him squarely in all eyes. "I understand… I would have wanted out of there, too. You did what you had to do."

"But that was at first, when I thought I had to… I meant it when I said I was on your side."

"I know. And you stepped up when it mattered the most and for that I thank you."

"I hate to break up the love fest," Derek injected, "but we've got more pressing issues here."

"Yeah, you're right," Max said, "first and foremost, where's Sam, is she okay, did she make it back?"

By now the Assembly throng, their exit out of Nemesis completely blocked, had turned their angry gaze towards the threesome, their voices echoing in fits of rage.

"Oh Max, how on earth do you manage to do this?" Derek sighed. "From bad to worse and then worser?"

The trio grouped together, backs to each other, the angry mob of thwarted Barghests, Wereboars, and Hobgoblins approaching fast. The three banded even more tightly together, each facing outwards.

"What's the weapons count?" Max shouted.

"Just the one measly Extractor," Humphries cried out above the shouts. "And it's nothing against this many of them."

Bah-bah-bah-baaaah!! A trumpet-like sound echoed throughout the Assembly arena. In the distance, a flock of winged creatures filled the air.

"It's Sam!" Derek shouted triumphantly. "And Johannes! And he's brought all his men with him!" Suddenly the Assembly floor lit up with Extractor fire, as Sam, Johannes, Paschal, and the other monks dove their narks toward the Assembly throng surrounding Max, Derek, and Humphries.

"Here, Max, catch!" Sam shouted out, tossing a spare Extractor gun his way, while dismounting the Nark.

Max caught it as Johannes' men jumped from their Narks and formed a circle around Max, Derek, and Humphries.

"H-how did you do it?" Max yelled above the roar of the approaching Nemenites and the high-pitched zinging of the Time Extractors bouncing off the walls.

"We knew that Narks were trained to deliver intruders to the Assembly floor," Johannes replied, "plus Sam here turns out to be a bit of a Nark whisperer, must have been something we missed in the manuscript."

"Wow!" Derek exclaimed. "Maybe I'll take up reading, I thought it was just a fad!"

"Ow!" Max recoiled as a shot bounced off his Extractor and grazed his hand. "Humphries! What's the best way out of here?"

"Actually? There was a way," Humphries yelled back pointing upwards at the ceiling of the Assembly, "until you managed to permanently seal it off."

"What!" Derek screamed. "You mean there's no back door to this place, no secret exit? Isn't that against fire code regulations or something?"

"There is one way," Johannes stated solemnly. "You can drink the *prana.*"

"Yeah! Now that's what I'm talking about!" Derek exclaimed loudly, letting off another rat-a-tat volley of Extractor beam shots directly into the angry crowd. "Let's do what these rat finks were planning to do and get the heck outta here!"

By now the group had worked its way back into one of the Assembly entrances, laying down a steady line of fire against the approaching mob.

"But the gate's been sealed?" Max questioned intently.

"But that gate was built long ago, and it was designed to contain the Nemenites from leaving all at once, en masse, your way will need to be the way of the Boggart, through dreams," Johannes continued. "With enough *prana,* you and your friends can safely return—just ask your Boggart friend."

Max turned to Humphries. "Is that true, Hump?"

"It just depends," he replied.

"Depends on what?" Derek demanded. "Are you holding out on us again?"

"It's risky, Max," Humphries shouted, now behind one of the arena walls, near the seating and the feeding troughs, still filled with the abandoned prana.

"Why is it risky?" asked Sam, ducking down low to avoid the incoming shots.

"Because you can only enter when someone is actively dreaming, or at least daydreaming about you. As long as they are in a semi trance state, and thinking of you, it should work. Otherwise…"

"Otherwise, what?"

"Otherwise, you won't make it, you'll be caught in the transition and end up suspended, like what you call purgatory, waiting for who knows how long.

The approaching hordes of screeching Barghests, Wereboars, and Changelings were upon them now, attempting to climb over the one wall separating them.

"The question is whether anyone still has dreams left, specifically dreams of you," Humprhies said, taking his eyes off the approaching danger to give Max one last look.

"They're closing in, Sir Max," Johannes announced. "You must make your decision quickly."

"But what about you, Johannes, and Pasquel. And your men? We have to stay and help fight!" Max stated.

"No one in your world has dreamed of us for a long time, Max, so we have no entry back to the world. But then, it is no longer our world. You've done more than anyone could expect, and for that we owe you our gratitude. What we can do is stay here and fight until you're safely home. And to make sure this doesn't happen again."

"And you, Humphries, what about you?"

"Are you kidding, Max? These guys are going to need an informant, and who better qualified than me? Besides, I know all the back tunnels and where the extra Extractors are hidden. We'll keep Nemesis busy for eons."

Zang! Another bolt came whizzing by. Meanwhile, the smell of grunting Wereboar breath was coming at them over the wall.

"C'mon, Max, Sam!" Derek shouted, scooping up a handful of the *prana* puddled in a nearby feeding trough. "It's our last chance."

Max looked up at Johannes and then over to Humphries. "If I make it, I'll dream about you—both of you, so don't give up hope!"

"We won't, Max," Johannes said, shaking Max's hand firmly.

"Fleshies!" Humphries exclaimed in exasperation. Max hugged Humphries hard around his oversized neck and then turned to run to Derek.

ZZZZzzzzaaaap! Max fell sharply to the ground.

"C'mon, Max! Get up, drink this and let's get going!" Derek urged.

Max half-crawled, half-pulled himself to the side of the trough. The gooey fluorescent purple *prana* pulsated in his hand as he lifted it to drink. He looked over to see Derek eagerly gulping handfuls of the thick, mysterious mixture. Sam made a puckered-up face and then did her best to scoop small handfuls in her mouth in quick succession. The chamber rang with Extractor fire and Max could hear shouting right behind him, and the sensation of something trying to grab hold of his feet.

Then it happened.

The trough he was drinking from began to spin, slowly at first, and then increasingly fast. Max grabbed hold, as if on a high-speed merry-go-round. While it spun, images began flashing all around him. All he could see were bits and pieces, fragments of faces, muffled voices, and then emptiness.

Emptiness and silence.

No one thought of me. I didn't make it. I must be dead.

Max felt nothing, only a strange heaviness, as if floating atop a warm ocean current on a moonless night. It seemed strange, not eerily strange, but peacefully strange.

"So what's it like to be dead, Max?"

"W-who's that?"

"Obviously it's someone who can talk to the dead," the voice replied.

"Zadkiel!" Max exclaimed. "You're back… or am I back? I'm not quite sure which. Uh, where are we?"

"Let's just say we're on pause for now."

"Well, it's so good to see you! You were so right about things not being as they seemed. It was crazy back there! I had everything wrong—the reason for the stone, Humphries being on their side—well, sort of, but not really, if that makes any sense. And every time I tried to figure things out, they just got worse. I almost blew the whole deal."

"But you didn't."

"But I could have and then what would have happened? We're talking about the entire planet here… Earth… people… lives… humanity… Empyrean! All that could have just, just…"

"Just what Max?"

"I don't know… I don't want to think about it."

"Then perhaps it's time to stop thinking," Zadkiel suggested. "You said it yourself, it didn't help."

"Well, if I stop thinking, then how will I know what to do next?"

"Well, I guess that's just something you'll have to think about, Max."

"Zadkiel… hey, that's not fair! What happens next? You said we're on pause, the transition back through, right? I didn't make it, did I? No one thought of me, so I'm stuck in suspension.

"That all depends, Max, suspension is a funny thing, like when you suspend judgment, it means you keep your mind open, you observe, you watch and see where things lead and how things work out. It's all in how you think about it, Max…" And with that, Zadkiel was gone.

CHAPTER 32

*B*ZZZZZZZ! The alarm rang out of the room and into the hallways.

"Nurse! Give me the crash cart!" the doctor ordered gruffly.

"Clear!"

ZAAAAAAPP!

"We have a pulse again," the nurse shouted. "He's showing some color."

Max sat up slowly, grabbing the wooden handles of the cushioned chair he found himself seated in. Still groggy, he rubbed his eyes as the fuzzy outlines of a hospital room emerged through a thinning mental fog. He peered intently to make out a hospital bed in the distance with a patient lying stretched out on it, surrounded by an assortment of medical staff, beeping monitors and flashing lights.

"Good. Make sure to monitor his oxygen, BP and call me if anything changes."

"Yes, doctor," the nurse replied. "It's just that he keeps trying to come to, he keeps calling out someone's name, sounds like Mark or Mack or something, but I'm not sure…"

The busy nursing staff made some adjustments to monitors and then turned to leave.

"Oh my! Where did you come from?" the surprised nurse said as she spied Max. "I didn't even see you sitting here a minute ago, you must have snuck in from out of nowhere! Are you family to this gentleman? Is he your grandfather?"

Before Max could even attempt to answer, the nurse cut him off.

"Here, I have to step out to get some supplies," she stated matter-of-factly. "Just be aware, visiting hours are almost over, so you can stay a couple more minutes; meanwhile, be sure to call me if he wakes up, okay?" With that, she pointed to a call button attached to the hospital bed. Max nodded at her instructions, before getting up slowly and approaching the patient's bed. There he paused for a second, examining a face that was barely visible beneath the maze of gauze, tape, and tubes. The patient's chest rose and fell sporadically before settling into a slow and steady rhythm. Max leaned in to study the man's weathered features when he felt a familiar firm grasp.

"Max! Max… is that you?"

"Professor? Professor Gutt?" Max's mouth dropped in amazement. "How could it be? How did I end up back here in your…"

"Max, thank God it's you. I've been so worried. Even when I was under, when I was unconscious, I knew someone had to be there for you, so I held on as best I could. I held on to the very thought of you, Max. I just knew you could do it." The professor attempted to reach over and place his thin hand on Max's shoulder, wincing in pain as he did so.

"Don't, don't move, Professor. Just relax, I can call the nurse."

"No need, Max. No need at all. I'm sure I'll be fine now. I think it will all be fine…"

"Professor? Professor?"

An alarm sounded as lights began to blink and flash. "His vitals are dropping again!" a nurse called out as she ran back into the room dropping a tray of supplies along the way. "I'm sorry, young man, but you're going to have to leave," she said to Max.

"Max, wait!" The Professor struggled to speak.

"Sir, I'm afraid you can't talk right now, you have to rest," the nurse insisted.

"Your father… I dreamt of him as well, both of you were together… he's…"

"I'm afraid we don't have much time—you must leave now." And with that, the nurse pulled the curtain shut around the Professor, blocking him from view.

"Don't have much time!" The nurse's words hit Max like a sickening punch to the stomach. He glanced back at the Professor. The doctor had come back in to apply the paddles again, and the nurse shook her head as if to admit defeat.

"Not much time…" Max repeated to himself again. *"I've got to find Sam and Derek. There must be someone, anyone, thinking of them, dreaming of them."*

Max raced down the hospital corridors and burst out the front doors. Startled visitors jumped to the side as he bolted down Elmgrove Avenue and headed directly for Sam's house. Max glanced at his watch… 4:45 p.m., nearly the exact time they had met at Sam's house. *But was it the same day? The same week?* Max's thoughts tumbled like a rushing torrent through his mind. As he passed by the school, a couple of classmates were leaving down the front steps.

"Hey! Have either of you seen Sam or Derek? Anybody?"

Nothing but blank stares greeted his questions. Max turned the corner, his heart now racing. Saving time, he cut through the school parking lot when he bumped into…

"Max?"

"Ms. Stolty! Ms. Stolty… have you seen Derek? Has he been here today?"

"Of course, Max. Calm down! He was here earlier today with you! Don't you remember? Or did you forget that too, Mr. Daydreamer? I've got to tell you Max, this is all getting pretty serious. If you're ever going to amount to anything you're going to have to start to apply yourself… Max? Max!"

He was already gone. He covered the distance from school to Sam's house on Adelphi Street in a matter of minutes. The cars were gone, the doors locked—obviously Sam's dad was still at work. Max searched under the doormat for the spare key he knew she kept there. Unable to find it, he banged on the window. "Sam, Sam, are you in there? C'mon! Where are you?"

Just then Sam's dad pulled up, and climbing up the stairs, shouted up to Max.

"Hey Max, what's the matter, are you alright? Why are you asking about Sam? She should be inside."

"Yeah, I know, but I guess she… uh, can't hear me? Say, did you happen to be sleeping at work, or maybe thinking about Sam while you nodded off on your way home?" Max asked, trying to appear normal.

"Max, are you sure you're alright? I'm sure she's fine," he replied, now getting out his keys and opening the door. "Sam! It's Dad. Sam, you here?"

Nothing.

"Odd, she's usually back home by now," Sam's dad mused. "Can't imagine where she would be at this time…"

"Right here, Dad," Sam replied, coming around the corner from her bedroom.

"Sam!" they both replied at once, her father then giving an odd glance at Max.

"I didn't realize you were such close friends," Sam's father said with a curious look. "Here, let me get you two a couple of sodas." With that he scurried off.

"Sam! You scared the bejeezus out of me," Max exclaimed. "Who would have known that it would be midafternoon; there was no way your dad could have possibly been sleeping or dreaming of you… I don't get it?"

Sam gave Max a broad smile and then looking down, nodded at the cat wrapped snugly in her arms. "Apparently something was dreaming of me… right, Mr. Jitters?"

Relieved, Max fell back in a living room chair. "That just leaves Derek, and I'm even less certain. His folks are away on vacation, so he was staying with us. Let's try his house first." Not wasting a second, Sam and Max made their way back down the steps and off again, racing towards Derek's place. The houses whirled by.

He fought for me, but how do I fight for him, Max thought. *There's nothing more I know to do, no Plan B, C or D.*

They turned the corner to Derek's house, both winded. The lights were off. No cars in the driveway.

"My place, I don't know where else we could look," Max insisted.

They covered the short distance to Max's house in a matter of minutes and sprinted through the door.

"Derek! Derek!" they both shouted, searching the living room, garage, and back porch.

"Hold it down! Hold it down! What's all the commotion?" came the familiar voice of Uncle Owen. "What are you two all fired up about?"

"Uncle Owen," Max blurted out, between breaths. "Ask him Sam," he said, trying to regain his voice.

"Have you seen Derek? We're looking for him. It's really, really important."

"Well, I'm sure it is, everything is at that age. But no, unfortunately, I haven't seen hide nor hair of young Derek. I think he's gone off somewhere, who knows where…" his voice trailed off.

"Gone?"

"Sam, what are we going to do? What do we tell Derek's parents?"

"Wait!" came the voice from the living room. Uncle Owen had returned. "Funny that you should mention Derek, because I just had the weirdest dream just now, and he was in it! He was going through our fridge, you know how he does, eating plates of leftover spaghetti and a whole box of Twinkies. I mean, doesn't that sound a bit like Derek?" he laughed to himself, now heading back to the living room to complete his nap. "It's a bit over the top, but then again, you know how that kid can eat…"

"Wait!" both Max and Sam said at once. "You were dreaming of him?"

"Well, yeah. But you know how I get those strange dreams. Like the one I told you about last week when I imagined these mutant creatures were trying to… Max? Sam?"

Max was already racing around the corner of the living room, down the hallway and into the kitchen with Sam in close pursuit. He stopped abruptly. All he could see was the refrigerator door open, the light casting an outline around a familiar figure.

"Why don't you guys ever have anything decent to eat in here? It's all… yuck! Health food!"

"Derek!" Max jumped the last three feet and landed squarely on Derek's back, wrapping both arms tightly around his neck and knocking them both to the linoleum floor. Sam watched, a grin running from ear to ear, shaking her head.

"You made it! You really made it!"

"Yeah, but I've got to admit that your Uncle Owen has some pretty strange dreams. Although the stuff in his dream-fridge is way better than this crap!"

"That's it? That's all you have to say about getting back here?"

"Listen, Max," Derek turned and grasped Max's face, placing it squarely between his open palms, as if to gain his undivided attention.

"I have no idea what to think about any of this," he half shouted, half whispered. Heck, we could still be in some dream! I just know I'm back home—we're back home! That's good enough. I don't want to jinx it. Heck, if we wrote this up in creative writing, we'd get a big ol' F for being Freaks, or worse yet, put in a psych ward."

Sam rolled her eyes up in her head, nodding. "I'll second that motion! Mum's the word as far as I'm concerned."

"All I know is that I'm going to think twice about signing on to any more of your harebrained schemes from here on out."

Max paused to take it all in. "I guess you're right. Maybe we just keep all this to ourselves. Maybe no one really needs to know."

"Know what?" Derek shook his head, a grin slowly spreading across his face. "The fact that we saved the freakin' planet?"

Max laughed; Sam half snorted. "Yeah, something like that. C'mon!" Max said, standing back up and leaning over to give Derek a hand up. "What do you say we get back to worrying about the really important stuff?"

"You mean like Stolty's midterm tomorrow?" Sam replied.

"Yeah," Max laughed. "Earth-changing stuff like that."

Derek reached over to close the refrigerator door. "There wasn't anything worth eating in there, anyway. Besides, that reminds me, I know just the perfect snack right now." With that, Derek opened the backpack Max was still wearing, pulling out a shiny apple, the size of a grapefruit. "Did you really think I would leave without snagging one of these?" he said, tossing it in the air for good measure. Derek took several big bites out of the glowing fruit, polishing off all but the remaining core in under a minute.

"I think for once my appetite is finally gone!" Derek exclaimed.

"Really? We'll just have to see about that," said Max with a suspicious look.

Derek laughed in agreement, and sliding open the kitchen sink window, he tossed the remaining apple core into the backyard garden, shiny wet seeds flying loose and landing in the moist, fertile soil.

"Everything will be back to normal soon," he sighed.

"Yeah," Max agreed. "In no time at all."

The End

ACKNOWLEDGMENTS

Writing is something you do because you need to do it, sort of a compulsive therapy if there is such a thing. As a child I could not quit asking my mother "What if?" followed by a slew of never-ending questions. That curiosity eventually found expression on paper. I would feel much worse about putting her through such an ordeal, except that the writing gene came from her, so in a sense it was well deserved.

Beyond my beloved mother, I owe a debt of gratitude to a few other folks, but none whatsoever to my first-grade teacher, for reasons that should be obvious from reading this book. The patience award goes to Kimberly Miller, my personal assistant, who for many months dutifully mailed manuscripts and picked up rejection letters. To Tim Grundmann, a man of many talents, who edited my first draft. To my editor extraordinaire, Jennifer Rees, the iron hand in a velvet glove, for providing the encouragement and tough love necessary to take a project from concept to completion. To Lisa Stallings for an extra set of keen eyes in the final stretch. And to my wife Michelle, my biggest fan, who thinks I'm wasting time writing this when I could be working on my next book.

But most of all, I owe a debt to readers like you, who inspire me to keep wondering "What if…"

Made in United States
North Haven, CT
18 March 2024